JUSTICE OF THE GUN
THE CROCKETTS' WESTERN SAGA: 10

ROBERT VAUGHAN

WOLFPACK
PUBLISHING
— EST 2013 —

WOLFPACK PUBLISHING
— EST 2013 —

Published in the United States by Wolfpack Publishing, Las
Vegas

Wolfpack Publishing
5130 S. Fort Apache Road 215-380
Las Vegas, NV 89148
wolfpackpublishing.com

Paperback ISBN 978-1-64734-517-4
eBook ISBN 978-1-64734-516-7

JUSTICE OF THE GUN

Chapter One

Will and Gid Crockett had just delivered a hundred Missouri mules to the US Army at Fort Bliss, Texas, and they were invited to have dinner with Lt. Colonel Hopkins, who was the Chief Quartermaster of the fort.

"I suppose you two are a little uncomfortable being surrounded by all these blue uniforms," Colonel Hopkins said.

"Why should we be uncomfortable?" Gid asked.

"Well, after all, you did fight for the South, didn't you? I've been led to believe that you were with Quantrill."

"I thought the war was over," Gid said. "I haven't been misinformed, have I?"

"No, Mr. Crockett, you have not been misinformed, the war is over, and I apologize for my comment."

"That's all right," Gid said as he was cutting his meat. "If I had seen you back then, I would have shot you."

Hopkins got a shocked look on his face, then the shock gave way and he chuckled. "Indeed, you may well have."

"But think about it, Gid. If we had killed him, we would have missed this fine dinner," Will said.

As they were eating, a private approached the table, and saluted Colonel Hopkins.

"Private, would you mind telling me what is so important that you would interrupt our dinner?" Hopkins said, rather harshly.

"General Parker sent me here, sir. I have a telegram for Mr. Crockett."

"Which one of us?" Will asked.

"I don't know, sir. I was just told Mr. Crockett."

"I'll take it," Will said.

"How would anyone know how to find you, to send you a telegram?" Hopkins asked.

"It's from John Abernathy, a friend of ours," Will said as he glanced at the telegram. "We stopped by his ranch to see him when we were on the way down here, so he knew where we were headed."

"What is it?" Gid asked.

"He wants us to come by the ranch again."

"We were going to do that anyway, weren't we?"

"Yes, but I think he has something specific in mind." Will showed Gid the telegram.

FRIEND NEEDS HELP WITH JOB YOU DO BEST

6

STOP COME TO LONG TRAIL NOW STOP JOHN
ABERNATHY.

When Will and Gid arrived at Long Trail Ranch, they
were met by John and Ethyl Abernathy's daughter, Julia.

"Hello, Will, Gid. It's good to see you again," Julia said
as she ran toward them. A year earlier, Julia had been
kidnapped and held for ransom by Silas King and his gang
of outlaws. She was rescued by the Crockett brothers.

"Daddy is waiting for you, go on in. I'll take care of
your horses."

"Thanks, pretty girl," Gid said.

Julia blushed as she took the reins of the horses and
led them to the stable.

"Will, Gid, thanks for coming," John said, greeting the
brothers as they went into the "Big House" as the ranch
hands who worked on Long Trail Ranch called the Abernathy residence.

"What's up?" Will asked. "What's this job you spoke
about in the telegram?"

"I'd rather David Andrews tell you."

"And who's David Andrews?" Gid asked. "Do we
know him?"

"He's the president of the Reeves County Cattlemen's
Association."

"Problems with cattle thieves?"

"It's much worse than that. But I don't want to say any more about it. David will be able to lay it out for you much better than I can."

"But," Ethyl said, "you'll stay for supper and spend the night won't you? You can see Mr. Andrews in the morning. Besides that I'll ask Fred and Leah to come for supper as well, and I know you'll want to visit with them."

"You know you don't have to ever twist my arm to get me to eat," Gid said.

Leah and Fred Bell arrived at the Abernathys late in the afternoon. Fred, who had been with Will and Gid during the war, was what one could call a reformed outlaw. He had joined the Silas King gang and was with the gang when they stopped a train—one that just happened to have Will and Gid on board. Together, the Crocketts had thwarted the attempted robbery, and in the process had shot Fred Bell, thus stopping his life of crime before it had a chance to blossom. While Fred was recovering from his gunshot wound, he met Leah.

In the meantime, Will and Gid had been hired to find Julia Abernathy after she had run away to marry a man whom she trusted. That man, proved to be a member of the King gang, and a plot was hatched to hold Julia for ransom. With the help of Leah and Fred, Julia was rescued and the charges against Fred were never filed.

Very soon thereafter, Leah and Fred were married and were now very prominent citizens in the community, Fred operating a furniture-making operation, and Leah, along with Julia, taught in a school that John provided for the children of the hands who worked on the ranches in the area.

It was a happy meal, sharing stories of their mutual past, and catching each other up on the happenings since last they saw each other. There was no mention of the reason Will and Gid had been summoned, and though Will wanted to ask Fred if he knew anything about it, he refrained, out of respect for John's wishes.

As Will and Gid Crockett rode into Toyah the next morning, it was a subconscious act on their part to examine every roof top, every break between the buildings, as well as the men going about their normal business. Will and Gid, who had once ridden with Quantrill, had spent their time since the war atoning for that. Now, they were paladins of the plains, an enemy of evil, selling their guns, but not their souls, to people in need. It was for that reason that John Abernathy had sent for them.

"There's the Cattlemen's Association office just ahead," Will said.

Reaching the building Will had pointed out, the two men looped the reins around the hitching rail, then stepped inside.

An attractive young woman was sitting behind a desk, and she greeted the two men with a pretty smile.

"May I help you gentlemen?"

"I don't know," Gid said. "What do you want to help us do?"

"What?" the young woman asked, clearly confused by Gid's response.

Will laughed. "Don't mind my little brother."

"Your *little* brother?" the woman asked her confusion deepening as she looked at the two men. Gid was a full head taller and fifty pounds heavier than Will, the additional weight being muscle.

"Well, he's younger, and there was a time when he was smaller," Will explained. "I'm Will Crocket, and this is my brother, Gid. John Abernathy has led us to believe that Mr. Anderson may be expecting us."

The expression on the young woman's face turned from one of confusion to understanding. "Yes, yes, indeed he is," she said with a smile. "Wait just a moment and I'll tell him you're here."

When Will and Gid entered the office there were two men in conversation. One of the men they recognized as Sheriff Wallace. They had worked with Sheriff Wallace when they rescued Julia from the Silas King gang. The other man, who was nicely dressed, rose and came to greet them, then pulled up a chair for each of them.

"Gentlemen, it's a pleasure to meet you. Your reputation is far and wide."

Gid raised his eyebrows. "Our reputation? I hope it's good."

"It's as good as my word," Sheriff Wallace said, with a smile.

"Oh, yes, Mr. Crockett. You come highly recommended, not only by the good sheriff here, but also by John Abernathy, who I believe you know."

"Yes, he was gracious enough to put us up last night," Will said.

"John was most impressed with how you were able to successfully solve his problem here a while back."

"And we hope you can help us again," Sheriff Wallace said.

"I don't believe John spelled out what has been happening here," Andrews said, "but we have a band that has been rustling our cattle—only a few head at a time, so the Cattlemen's Association has been letting it slide I'm afraid."

"But now we have all the evidence we need to go after these murderers," Sheriff Wallace said.

"Wait a minute," Gid said. "There's a big difference between taking a few cows and calling somebody a murderer."

"Just about a month ago, murder is exactly what they did," Sheriff Wallace said. "They raided the Rocking P Ranch, waiting outside the house until sunup. Then they broke in on George Peterson and his family at breakfast. They killed Peterson and his sixteen-year-old son, outright, then they raped and killed Peterson's wife, and their fifteen-year-old daughter."

"Then they stole fifty head of prime beef," Anderson added. "George Peterson was a member in good standing of the Cattlemen's Association, and we aim to do what we can to catch these four men and we're ready to pay a pretty good piece of money if you can bring them in, one way or another."

"How do you know there were four?" Will asked.

"Oh, we know all right—we even know their names: Abner and Slim Newcomb, and their cousins, Bart and Clem Cassidy," Sheriff Wallace said.

"The state's offerin' a two hundred fifty-dollar reward for each of these men, and the Cattlemen's Association is prepared to match that, just to make certain that justice is done," Andrews said.

"Where did you get this information if everyone was killed?" Will asked.

Sheriff Wallace laughed. "There *were* five of them, but the Newcombs and the Cassidys decided they didn't want to share their bounty with anybody outside the family, so they shot one of their own, and left him to die. When a neighbor came by the Peterson place, he discovered that they were all dead, and then he found the wounded man still alive so he brought him in. Only the man didn't die. He's told us everything we needed to know about the outlaws, hoping that'll keep him from hanging."

"That's good," Will said. "He should be able to give us with some pretty good information."

"Listen, if you two are willing to go after these men, let me make you temporary deputies. It won't keep you from collecting the reward, but it will provide you with any legal cover should you need it."

"Where is this informant now?" Will asked. "Is he with a doc, or is he well enough to be in jail? And can we visit with him anytime soon?"

"It turns out his wound wasn't all that serious," Andrews said. "Martin Baker is in jail."

Will and Gid looked at each other.

"What did you say his name was?"

"Baker. Martin Baker," the sheriff replied.

"An ugly, runty-looking guy with a smashed in nose?" Gid asked.

"That pretty much describes him. Do you know him?"

Gid nodded. "Yeah, we know the son of a bitch. I'm the one that broke his nose."

"I'd like to talk to him," Will said.

"All right," Sheriff Wallace said. "Come along with me."

The sheriff took Will and Gid down to the jail.

"My prisoner is back here," he said as he led Will and Gid through a hallway to the back of the jail where there were two cells, only one of which was occupied.

"Here he is," the sheriff said. "I hope you can get somethin' else out of him."

Martin Baker was lying on his back his hands laced behind his head. He hadn't looked around when Wallace brought the Crocketts in, so he didn't know who was here.

"We need to talk to you, Baker," Will said.

"I've already talked."

"Not to us you haven't. Turn around here and look at me."

"Now why the hell would I want to do that?" Baker asked, though he was sitting up and turning around, even as he was responding. When he saw who was here to see him, his eyes grew large in surprise and sub-consciously, he put his hand to his nose.

"I'll be damn, if it ain't the Crocketts."

"What happened to you, Baker? You were never much more than a nasty drunk. How'd you go from there to murdering an entire family?"

"I didn't kill none of 'em,"

"You were there. One of Peterson's neighbors found

14

you lying in front of the house."

"And I was shot—shot in the back," Baker said. "I was half dead."

"You want to tell your side of the story?"

"I already told the sheriff all I know," Baker said. "They had me outside to keep watch. They said they was just going in to get some grub. I didn't have no idea they was goin' to kill ever'one, 'n when they come out, I called 'em on it. 'N that's when Clem Cassidy shot me. Are you gonna bring that son of a bitch in for shootin' a man in the back?"

"If we bring him in, it will be for killing four innocent people. As far as shooting you in the back, that's sort of extra," Gid said.

"Do you have any idea where they were going next?" Will asked. "Do they have some place to hole up for awhile?"

"If I tell you two, will you cut me loose?"

"That's for the judge to decide."

"Then I ain't sayin' nothin' at all. I figure that's about the only bargaining chip I got."

"All right, suit yourself," Will said, dismissively.

Chapter Two

Even as Will and Gid were talking to Martin Baker, Abner and Slim Newcomb and Bart and Clem Cassidy were riding into the small town of Brown Spur, Texas. They stopped in front of the Boots Saloon.

"You sure this is a smart move?" Clem asked. "I mean, shouldn't we just do our job and be gone?"

"We don't get nobody lookin' at us this way," Bart said. "Anyone lookin' at us will just think we're four cowboys come into town for a drink."

"Yeah, but the only thing wrong with that is Brown Spur's the only town around here, so it's more 'n likely they know all the ranch hands within ten miles."

Bart chuckled. "All right, so we're comin' from twelve miles away lookin' for work. Besides, are you saying you don't want a drink?"

Clem smiled. "You know me, Bart. I'm always ready

for a drink."

Dismounting and looping their reins over the hitching rail, the four men went inside where they were greeted by a bargirl. Her welcoming smile showed the gap of a missing tooth, knocked out by a drunken cowboy.

"Damn, Hallie, what are you doing here?" Bart asked. "I thought you was workin' at the Ace High, up in Salcedo."

"I got out of that place, and decided to come to Brown Spur. And ain't you glad I did? Which one of you boys wants to come visit me first?"

"Not now, Hallie. We've got something we have to take care of first," Bart said. "Soon as we finish this drink."

The four men visited with Hallie for a few minutes more, then left the saloon.

Mark Lyons, who owned the bank of Salcedo, looked up as three men came into the bank. The town was small enough that he could recognize on sight, any of his customers, and he didn't recognize these three men. He greeted them with a smile, thinking they might be potential customers.

"What can I do for you gentlemen?" Lyons asked."

"We'd like to make a withdrawal," Bart said.

The smile left Lyons's face when he saw guns appear in their hands.

"Get your hands up," Bart said as he shoved a sack

toward Lyons. "Fill that with everything you've got."

"Give them the money, Mr. Wheeler," Lyons said.

Hodge Wheeler took all the money from the cash drawer and began putting it in the bag.

"A hunnert 'n sixty dollars? That's all you got?" Bart asked as he watched Wheeler handle the money.

"Sir, as you can see, the drawer is empty," Wheeler said.

"Empty your safe, too."

Wheeler looked over at Lyons.

"Empty the safe for them, Mr. Wheeler."

Wheeler emptied the safe and gave them six hundred and forty more dollars.

"That's it?" Bart asked sharply. "That's all the money you got?"

"As you can see, sir, our safe is empty," Lyons said.

"What the hell kind of bank has only eight hundred dollars?"

"A very small bank, sir, like ours."

Bart smiled. "Well, now your bank is even smaller, ain't it?"

Hallie was watching as Bart, Clem and Abner came out of the bank, and mounted the horses Slim had been holding for them. They galloped out of town.

"Hold up!" Lyons shouted, running out into the street. "The bank's been held up!"

Sheriff Boyer came out of his office then, drawn out by Lyons' shouting. "What is it, what happened?"

"The bank was robbed!" Lyons yelled.

"Did you recognize any of them?" the sheriff called as he hurried toward the bank.

"Not a one of them."

"Did anybody recognize them?" he asked looking around at the assembled crowd.

There were a lot of blank stares and shaking of heads, as no one claimed to have recognized any of the robbers.

"All right, I'm going to form a posse. Anyone who wants to join, meet me at my office in fifteen minutes, mounted, armed, and ready to go."

Six hours later, the posse returned, empty-handed and dejected.

"I thank you men for comin' along with me," Sheriff Boyer said. "I'm just real sorry we didn't catch up with the sons of bitches."

After the posse broke up a few of the men went into the Boots Saloon.

"I seen you boys comin' back," one of the saloon patrons said. "Didn't look to me like you caught anybody."

"We caught a lot of dust, is what we caught," one of the posse men said. "I been thinkin' for the last hour how good a beer would taste."

"I tell you what, since you boys went out on the posse, the first beer is free," the bartender said.

"Any luck in findin' out who them boys was?" one of other patrons asked.

"We don't have an idea in hell who they was," one of posse men replied.

"Iffen we had knowed who they was, that might of give us some clue that we could 'a used to find 'em, but we didn't have nothin' at all to go on."

Hallie was listening to the conversation without joining it. After a while, she left the saloon quietly, so as not to draw any attention to herself. She would just as soon nobody know what she had in mind.

Sheriff Boyer had just poured himself a cup of coffee when Hallie stepped into his office.

"Howdy, Hallie? Is some cowboy getting rough with you?"

"No," Hallie said. "Nothing like that. It's just that, well, I have something to tell you."

"Oh?"

"I'll tell you, but I don't want it gettin' out all over town that I was the one that said somethin'."

Sheriff Boyer poured another cup of coffee then handed it to Hallie. "Why don't you sit down and tell me what's on your mind."

"I know who them men was that held up the bank."

"You do?" Sheriff Boyer said, shocked by the declaration. "How do you know them?"

"They used to be right good customers of mine when I worked at the Ace High Saloon in Salcedo. Today, before they held up the bank, they come in the Boots, 'n had a couple of drinks, 'n visited with me.

"Then, when I heard all the noise about the bank bein' robbed 'n all, I come outside to see what was goin' on. That's when I seen 'em."

"All right, tell me who it was that you saw."

"It was the Newcomb brothers, Abner and Slim, and their cousins, Bart and Clem Cassidy."

"Damn!" Sheriff Boyer said. "I just got news on them." He pulled a sheet of paper from his desk drawer. "Yes. Them's the bastards who murdered a whole family over in Reeves County."

Chapter Three

Thirty miles away, in Toyah, Will and Gid were in the sheriff's office, when the Western Union boy came in with a telegram.

"This just came in. It's for you, Sheriff," he said as he handed the sheriff the telegram.

Sheriff Wallace tipped the boy a nickle, then opened the yellow envelope. "I'll be damn," he said.

"What is it, Sheriff?" Will asked.

The sheriff held the telegram out so Will and Gid could read it. "These are the same men we want you to find for us."

BANK OF BROWN SPUR ROBBED TODAY BY NEWCOMBS AND CASSIDYS.

"They do stay busy, don't they?" Sheriff Wallace said.

"Not for long," Will replied.

"I beg your pardon?"

"We're going to put them out of business."

Will and Gid's next stop was Brown Spur, Texas. There were no more than a dozen buildings in the town, the largest being the Boots Saloon. The second largest was the bank. There were only two people in the bank: Mark Lyons, the owner, and Hodge Wheeler, the teller.

"Four of them, there were," Lyons said. "But only three of them came into the bank."

"How do you know for a fact, who they were?" Will asked.

"The sheriff said Hallie identified them."

"Hallie?" Gid questioned.

"She's a bar girl down at Boots."

"And how does she know them?"

Lyons shrugged his shoulders. "You'll have to ask her that."

"How much money did they get?" Gid asked.

"Only eight hundred dollars," Lyons said.

"So, they didn't get any money from the safe?"

"They got all the money from the safe," Lyons said.

"Oh?"

Lyons smiled. "That is from the operating capital safe. The main safe, which we don't advertise that we have, has over eight thousand dollars in it. We try to keep about ten per cent of our cash on hand in the operating capital safe."

Gid smiled and nodded. "That seems like a smart move."

"Thank you," Lyons said, beaming under the compliment. "I thought of that little trick myself."

"Well, it seems to have served your depositors quite well," Will said. "And now, Little Brother, what do you say we make the acquaintance of Miss Hallie?"

"And maybe we could grab a beer as well," Gid added.

There were six men in the saloon, seven counting the bartender. Four of the patrons were at one table, two were at another. In addition to the seven men, there was one woman, a bar girl, the dissipation of time and toil having its effect on her. She was standing at the far end of the bar.

"What can I get for you fellers?" the bartender asked.

"We'll each have a beer," Will said, then he and Gid glanced down toward the bar girl.

"Excuse me, Miss," Will called out to her. "Do you suppose if my brother and I bought you a drink, you'd share a table with us?"

The bar girl smiled, showing the gap of a missing tooth.

"You bet I would, darlin'," she replied.

The bartender poured a drink, then slid the glass down to her. She picked it up, then flashed another gap-toothed smile toward Will and Gid. "This way, cowboys," she said, leading them toward an empty table.

"Are you Hallie?" Will asked.

24

"I sure am. Have you heard of me, honey?"

"We're told that you're the only one who was able to identify the bank robbers."

"That's right," Hallie replied with pride. "I'm the one who recognized them."

"How is it that you know them?" Gid asked.

"Oh, honey, when I worked the Ace High in Salcedo, they were my finest customers. But I never knowed they would do something like hold up a bank."

"That's not all they did," Will said. He told Hallie about the four men slaughtering an entire family near Toyah.

"Yes," Hallie said, visibly upset with the news. "Sheriff Boyer told me about that, and I'm so sorry to say I know them bastards."

"Do you have any idea where they might have gone?"

"I think I heard 'em say somethin' about the Apache Mountains, but I ain't sure, 'cause I wasn't really listenin' to 'em. I was just tryin' to get 'em to buy me a drink."

Will smiled. "I understand, Hallie, but thank you for what you've told us. You've been a big help."

Will and Gid's next stop was the Sheriff's office.

"Yes, sir, what can I do for you boys?" Sheriff Boyer asked.

Will was carrying a letter of identification from Sheriff Wallace, and he gave it to Boyer.

Mark,

These are the Crockett brothers, Will and

Gid. They are the men who helped me shut down the Silas King gang. As I'm sure you know, we have our own problems with the Newcombs and the Cassidys, they having murdered the Peterson family. Since you will be looking for them for bank robbery, and we are looking for them for murder, it might be good for us to join forces. Please give these two good men all the coopera-tion and help you can.

Larry Wallace

Sheriff, Reeves County

"If Larry vouches for you, I'll be glad to cooperate with you," Sheriff Boyer said, handing the letter back to Will. "Whatever you need, I'll see what I can do."

Back in Toyah, the town Will and Gid had just left, there was nobody in the sheriff's office at the moment. Deputy Phillips, who was on duty, had left a few minutes earlier to get the prisoner's supper. With the deputy gone, Baker initiated his escape plan. He had saved a tin of tomatoes from a meal he had been given several days ago. He had crushed the tomatoes and hidden the can under his bed for several days, letting the juice thicken. Retrieving the can, he put his finger in the substance and decided it was at just the right consistency to carry out his plan. First he dripped red spots on the floor. Then, he smeared his left wrist with the paste, and when he was satisfied that it looked like blood, he discarded the can in the chamber pot, and lay back on the bed, allowing his left arm to hang down over the red spots on the floor.

When he heard Deputy Phillips coming back into the jail, he turned his head toward the cell door, holding his eyes open, as if in a death stare. To add to the effect, he let his mouth fall open as well.

"Well, Baker," the deputy said. "You're goin' to like your supper tonight. Fried chicken, mashed potatoes, gravy, biscuits, what do you think?

"Did you hear me?"

Deputy Phillips stepped up to the jail cell and saw Baker lying on the bunk, eyes open and still, mouth open, and what appeared to be blood on his wrist.

"Holy hell, what have you done?" Phillips asked. Setting the food tray down, he opened the cell door, then rushed inside to examine Baker.

As the deputy leaned over the bunk, Baker managed to grab his pistol, then shoving it into Phillips' stomach pulled the trigger.

A moment later, eating a piece of chicken, Baker walked out of the jail cell, took the first horse he saw, and rode out of town.

Chapter Four

Slim Newcomb lay on top of a flat rock, looking back along the trail over which they had just come. They had discovered this morning that someone was trailing them and now, as Newcomb looked back over the trail, he saw the two riders, unerringly following them.

"Are they still there?" Abner asked.

"Yeah, they're not fallin' back."

"Where'd they come from? How'd they get on our trail?"

"I don't know who they are, or where they came from, I just know we ain't been able to shake 'em. Hell, I believe them bastards could track a speck of dust through a sand storm."

"What are we goin' to do about them sons of bitches if we can't get rid of 'em?" Abner growled.

Bart looked back in the direction from which the riders were coming. "All right, let's lead 'em up through that draw," he said, pointing ahead.

"That's a dead-end canyon," Clem pointed out. "Don't you 'member that? Hell, me 'n you was up here last year."

"I know that," Bart said, "but it's got two or three good places in there where we can hide. All we got to do is let 'em follow us in there, then pick 'em off like flies."

"What if they don't come in? What if they just stay back at the mouth of the canyon and wait us out?" Slim asked.

'Hell, they's only two of them, 'n they's four of us," Bart insisted. "If they don't come in, we'll just come out and get 'em."

"Bart's right," Abner said. "Let's just kill 'em, 'n get it over with."

"Come on, I know a perfect spot," Bart said. "Slim and I will take this side. Abner, you and Clem get on the other side. When they come in the canyon, we'll have them in a cross-fire."

"Shouldn't we have the same brothers on each side?" Clem asked.

"No," Bart said. "This way, we'll be sure to look out for one another."

"Bart's right," Abner said.

"All right, let's go on in there and take our positions in plenty of time to ambush them sons of bitches," Bart said.

"Right here," Bart said a short time later. "The draw is real narrow here, 'n look up there." He pointed to each side. "On both sides they's a place for us to get behind some rocks. We'll have cover, whilst they will be down here in the open, 'n it bein' so narrow here, they won't have no place to go." Bart chuckled. "Like I said, it'll be like pickin' 'em off like flies."

"What are we goin' to do about our horses?" Slim asked.

"Hell, slap 'em on the rump, 'n send them on through. This is a dead end, so they can't go nowhere. 'N when the shootin' starts, they'll be to scairt to come back. When it's all over, we can just go get 'em."

"What'll we do with them two after we kill 'em?"

"What do you mean, what'll we do with 'em? We'll just leave the bastards where they fall 'n let the critters have 'em."

"We better get on up there," Slim said.

Hitting the horses to drive them away, the four men separated into two on either side, then started climbing.

Neither Will nor Gid had ever been here before, but they had been in dozens of places just like this.

"Will, if I had to make a guess, I'd say this is a dead-end canyon."

The two brothers stopped at the mouth of the canyon and Will took a drink from his canteen while he studied it.

"You may be right, Little Brother."

"I don't think they'd come in here if they didn't already know whether it was a dead-end or not," Gid said, "which means if they know it's a dead-end, why would they come in here in the first place?"

"You know what I think? I think they know we're trailing them, and they want to draw us in, then set up an ambush for us."

Gid pulled his long gun out of the saddle holster. "Well, you know what they say. Forewarned is forearmed."

Carrying their rifles, Will and Gid started walking into the canyon, leading their horses. The horses' hooves fell sharply on the stone floor and echoed loudly back from the canyon walls. The canyon made a forty-five degree turn to the left just in front of them, so they stopped.

"I've got an idea," Will said. "Let's send the horses on ahead of us."

Slapping their horses on their rumps, they sent both animals bolting ahead.

Any question as to what the Newcombs and the Cassidys may have had in mind, was validated when the canyon exploded with the sound of gunfire as the outlaws opened up on what they thought would be their pursuers. Instead, their bullets whizzed harmlessly over the empty saddles of the two riderless horses, raising sparks as they hit the rocky ground, then whining off into empty space, echoing and re-echoing in a cacophony of whines and shrieks.

From his position just around the corner from the turn, Will located two of the ambushers, and getting Gid's attention, he pointed them out. Gid nodded in acknowledgement.

The two men were about a third of the way up the north wall of the canyon, squeezed in between the wall itself, and a rock outcropping that provided them with a natural cover. Or, so they thought.

The firing stopped and, after a few seconds of dying echoes, the canyon grew silent.

"Where the hell are they?" one of the ambushers yelled, and Will and Gid could hear the last two words repeated in echo down through the canyon.

Will studied the rock face of the wall just behind the spot where he had located two of them.

"Gid," he said loudly enough that only Gid could hear. "We can bounce our bullets off the rock wall behind them."

Gid nodded, then the two of them began firing. The rifles boomed loudly, the thunder of the detonating cartridges picking up resonance through the canyon and doubling, and re-doubling in intensity. Neither Will nor Gid were trying to aim at the two men, but were, instead, taking advantage of the position in which they had placed themselves.

"Clem, what the hell? Them bullets is . . . arrgh! Damn, I'm hit! I'm hit again."

The rock that they thought would be protecting them, had no effect at all. They were being hit by ricocheting bullets.

On the canyon floor, Will and Gid fired several rounds, knowing that the bullets were splattering against the rock wall behind the two men, fragmenting into deadly, whizzing, flying missiles of death. They emptied their rifles. Then, even before the echoes faded, they began reloading.

"Bart!" a strained voice called. "Bart! Can you hear me?"

"What is it?" another voice answered. This voice was from the opposite side of the narrow draw, half-way up on the facing wall.

"Bart, Slim, we're both killt."

"What?"

There was no answer.

"Clem?"

Silence.

"Abner!" the call was louder this time.

More silence.

"Clem? Abner? Answer us, you fools!"

But there was no answer.

"You son's of bitches, you killt our brothers!" Slim called.

Because of the echo effect, it was difficult to determine exactly where the remaining two outlaws were, but Will changed positions, then searched the opposite canyon wall.

There was silence for a long time, then, as he knew they would, his quarry began to get anxious. He saw first one, then the other pop up to have a look around.

"Slim, Bart," Will shouted, and the echo repeated the names.

"What do you want?"

"I want you to throw your guns down and give yourselves up," Will said.

"Why should we do that?"

For his answer, Will raised his rifle and shot at the wall just behind Slim and Bart, creating the same effect he had done with Abner and Slim. The only difference was that he shot only one round, and he placed it to give a demonstration of what he could do . . . not to kill.

"Son of a bitch!" one of the men shouted.

"We can take you out of there just the way we did your brothers," Will said. "Or we can play with you and let you wait up there until you run out of water. You didn't take your canteens with you, did you? We've got a little stream down here, and enough jerky to last us a week. You think you can last a week up there without food or water?"

Will was running a bluff. He couldn't see well enough

to determine whether they had their canteens or not. He would bet, however, that if they thought they would be able to set up the ambush and kill quickly, then they didn't think to take their canteens with them.

There was no response from the two men so, with a nod, Will and Gid fired a second time. The boom sounded like a cannon blast, and he heard the scream of the bullets, followed once more by a curse.

"By now you've probably figured out that we can make one bullet do the work of about ten," Will said. "And since there are two of us, that means two of our bullets can do the work of twenty. If we shoot again, we're going to put bullets where they can do the most damage . . . same as we did with the other two. You've got five seconds to give yourselves up, or die."

Will raised his rifle.

"No, wait! . . . *wait, wait, wait!*" the terrified word echoed through the canyon. "We're comin' down . . . *down, down, down!*"

"Throw your weapons down first."

Will and Gid saw hands appear, then pistols and rifles started tumbling down the side of the canyon, rattling and clattering until they reached the canyon floor.

"Put your hands up, then step out where we can see you," Will ordered.

The two men, moving hesitantly, edged out from

behind the rocky slab where they had taken cover. They held their hands over their heads.

"Come on down here," Will invited.

Stepping gingerly, the two climbed down the wall until, a moment later, they were standing in front of Will and Gid where Gid handcuffed each of them.

"What are you goin' to do with us?" Slim asked.

"I'm going to take you back to Toyah to stand trial," Will explained.

"How we goin' to ride like this?" Bart asked. "We can't stay in the saddle with our hands behind us like this. We'll fall off."

Gid smiled at them. "Well, try to stay on as long as you can, boys," he said, "and when you fall off, I'll help you on again."

Chapter Five

Two weeks later, five hundred miles east of Toyah, though still in Texas, four men, riding together, came into the town of Pettus. The fact that there were four of them together didn't warrant that much attention, as ranch hands would often come in, in clusters of four or five, or even more, sometimes to carry on some business for the brand they rode for, or sometimes to spend a little time in one of the saloons of Pettus. But Jess Felton, Julius Paxton, Edgar Kildeer, and Paddy O'Neal had something else in mind, this morning. One of the men, Jess Felton, stood out from the rest because of the way he looked.

Felton was a man of medium height and size, distinguished by his pock-marked face and a drooping left eye lid. The droop was the result of an old wound, suffered in a knife fight Felton had once had. The other man had cut the muscles over the eyelid, leaving Felton permanently disfigured. Felton had cut the other man's jugular vein, leaving him permanently dead.

Only one of the people who watched the four men ride into town had a second thought about it. He was standing in front of the Clark and Hopkins warehouse, having just delivered a wagon to them.

"What the hell are you doing here, Jess?" he asked quietly. "Whatever it is, I know you are up to no damn good. But what the hell else could I expect? You're no damn good yourself, and you never were any good."

Dan Evans spoke the words aloud, but he was speaking so quietly that nobody could hear him. He watched the five men ride down to the bank where three of them dismounted, passed the reins of their horses over to the two men who remained mounted, then went into the bank.

"Damn, this doesn't look good," Evans said, still speaking so quietly that no one could hear him. He started down the street toward the bank.

"Kildeer, you and O'Neal come with me," Felton said as he passed the reins of his horse to Paxton.

There were only three people in the bank, the teller, a woman customer, and the small boy standing beside her, holding his mother's hand. Felton, Kildeer, and O'Neal had their pistols drawn.

"This is a stick up!" Felton shouted.

"Oh!" the woman replied and reached down to put her hands on her son's shoulders, pulling him to her, protectively.

"All right, Mr. Bank Teller, open up your safe," Felton demanded, sticking his gun through the teller's window.

"I can't access the safe," the teller said. "Only the bank manager can do that," the teller replied in a voice that, because of his fear, was high pitched. The teller was also visibly shaking.

"How much do you have in the drawer?"

"One thousand, one hundred, seven dollars, and fifty-six cents," the teller said with the exactness of someone who kept up with every bank transaction.

"I'll take that," Felton said. "But you can keep the fifty-six cents," he added, with a sardonic chuckle.

The teller scooped the money out of the drawer, then with shaking hands, passed it through the window to Felton.

"Thank you, you've been just real helpful," Felton said as he pulled the trigger.

The teller fell backward with a black, oozing hole right in the middle of his forehead.

The woman screamed.

"Take care of the woman and the kid," Felton said as he was stuffing the money into his pockets.

Kildeer shot the woman; O'Neal shot the little boy.

"All right, let's get out of here," Felton said.

When the three men came out of the bank, there was an older, white-haired man standing in the street, right in front of the bank. He was looking right at them. Kildeer aimed his gun at the old man, but Felton reached over and grabbed Kildeer by the wrist, forcing the gun up, so that his shot went straight into the air.

"What the hell did you do that for?" Kildeer asked, surprised and irritated by Felton's action. "That old man could identify us."

"Let's go," Felton said, without replying to Kildeer's question.

Back in Toyah, Will and Gid had remained to be witnesses in the trial of Slim Newcomb and Bart Cassidy. The trial was for the murder of the George Peterson family, and for the bank robbery in Brown Spur.

"The truth is," Austin Dempster, the defense attorney said in his opening statement, "this trial shouldn't even be held here. You have no witnesses who can put my clients at the scene of the tragic murder of the Peterson family. The only witnesses who can testify as to any wrong doing, are witnesses to the bank robbery in Brown Spur. And that should be business better taken care of by the residents of Brown Spur."

"We have a signed statement from Martin Baker, who was not only a witness, but a participant in the tragic events that took place at the Peterson family ranch," the prosecutor, Robert Norton said.

"And just where is this witness?" Dempster asked. He looked around the court room. "Is he hiding somewhere? Has he crawled under your table? Where is he? If he is so instrumental to your case, why don't you call him to the stand?"

"Your Honor, I'm sure that, despite his theatrics, Mr. Dempster is well aware that Martin Baker escaped confinement, murdering Deputy Phillips in the process," Norton replied.

"Your Honor, I think my point has been made," Dempster said. "You can hardly declare the supposed comments of a witness in absentia. I'll have no opportunity for cross examination. I move that the so-called 'testimony' of this witness be excluded from any consideration."

"The witness made a sworn, signed statement, witnessed and attested to a notary public. I will let his testimony stand," the judge replied.

Neither Bart Cassidy, nor Slim Newcomb took the stand, and without a witness for the prosecution, there remained only the final arguments.

Once the court proceedings were concluded, the jury retired to find a verdict. It had been the highest profile trial ever held in Reeves County and feelings were running very deep because the murder of an entire family was the most heinous crime anyone had ever heard of. George Peterson was one of the business leaders of the community while his wife, Ellie Mae, was prominent in all the social and charity events. Their two children, Donnie and Lorena, were among the most popular students in the Toyah school.

Despite the lack of a prosecution witness, the jury, as expected, returned a verdict of guilty. Now their sentence, determined by the judge, was about to be announced. The judge turned his attention toward the defense table.

"Would counsel for the defense bring his clients to stand before the bench, please? Sheriff Wallace you will accompany them."

The two prisoners approached the bench, flanked by Sheriff Wallace on one side, and their defense attorney, Austin Dempster, on the other.

"Slim Newcomb, and Bart Cassidy, you have been tried by a jury of your peers for the despicable crime of murder, not of one person, not of two people, but of an entire family: a husband, a wife, a son and a daughter.

"You have been found guilty, and it now becomes my duty to pronounce sentence. Tomorrow morning, the crow of roosters will greet the rising sun, breakfast will be cooking in private homes and restaurants, and the wonderful aroma of bacon and coffee will perfume the air. Children, from infants to those in school, will be preparing to meet the new day in their young lives. Businessmen and workers will ensure that the wheels of commerce turn one more day.

"But you won't see any of this. When the sun rises, neither one of you will be here to embrace the joys of life, because it is my sentence that, before the sun sets tonight, you two are to be taken to a contrivance sufficient to support your weight, nooses to be placed around your neck, where you will hang suspended until death takes you from this earth, you low-life, miserable cretins."

The judge rapped his gavel on the bench. "This court is adjourned."

In anticipation of the judge's verdict, the gallows had already been constructed in the middle of what had been Center Street, but was renamed Peterson Street, in honor of the Peterson family.

Those who had been present for the trial, now gathered around the gallows to join the citizens of the town who had not attended the trial, but were already waiting, even before the two men were sentenced. Newcomb and Cassidy were brought directly from the courthouse to the gallows. Both men had their wrists handcuffed behind their backs as they were led up the thirteen steps to the gallows floor and the ropes dropped around their necks.

Both men declined a hood, and they stood there glaring at the crowd while the sheriff read the execution order. As soon as he finished, he nodded to the hangman, who pulled the lever opening the door that dropped them into eternity.

Those gathered to watch, applauded and cheered.

There was one witness to the execution who had kept himself hidden behind the corner of a building. He watched with interest as the prisoners were hurled into eternity.

"Shoot me, will you, you sorry sons of bitches," Martin Baker said quietly. He chuckled. "Well, guess what. I'm still alive, and you're dead."

Mounting his horse, Baker rode off while the citizens of the town were still celebrating.

From the Alamo Express of San Antonio

Justice served in Toyah, Texas

In the annals of Texas crime, there has seldom, if ever been a crime as heinous as the Peterson family slaughter. Five men, Abner and Slim Newcomb, and their cousins, Bart and Clem Cassidy, and Martin Baker, not related to any of the four, came upon a peaceful family as they were enjoying their breakfast and ruthlessly murdered George Peterson, his wife, Ellie Mae, and their two children, Donnie and Lorena.

Before leaving the scene, the four cousins, perhaps unwilling to share their ill-gotten gains, shot Martin Baker. Baker survived the shooting, and provided the names of the other four.

The four brigands may have thought they had gotten away with it, but they didn't take into account the skill, courage, and tenacity of the Crockett brothers, Will and Gid.

Two of the villains, Abner Newcomb and Clem Cassidy were killed during the initial confrontation between the Crockett brothers and the four outlaws. The remaining two, Slim Newcomb and Bart Cassidy were arrested by Will and Gid Crockett, the two brothers having been appointed temporary deputies, and brought to Toyah for trial.

Though the two men were ably represented by counsel, their guilt was es-

tablished beyond doubt and Sheriff Larry Wallace led the two men to the gallows where they paid the ultimate price for their transgressions.

The fifth man, Martin Baker, escaped, killing Deputy Phillips in the process, and remains at large.

Chapter Four

Five hundred miles away, in the sheriff's office at Tilden, Texas, Sheriff Tyrone McMurtry poured himself a second cup of coffee.

"Dan Evans was in Pettus when the bank was robbed, and he recognized Jess Felton when he and the others came out of the bank," Ty's deputy, Ward Haller said.

"Well, you're not really surprised, are you?" Ty asked. "Felton has been raising hell in LaSalle, McMullen, and Live Oak counties for the last six months."

"No one seems able to catch him," Ward said.

"I know, we have sheriffs and deputies out in all three counties, and even in those counties where he hasn't been active. But so far, the son of a bitch has managed to . . ." Ty stopped in mid-sentence.

"I'll be damn. I should have thought about them first. I know who might be able to take care of Felton for us."

"Who?"

"Did you read the story in the *Alamo Express*, about the men who murdered that whole family out in Toyah?"

"Yes, I read it. Why do you ask?"

"That nasty business was taken care of by the Crockett brothers. I'll get them to come to Tilden to help us."

Ward chuckled. "You're going to get the Crockett brothers to come to Tilden to help us catch Felton?"

"Yes."

"How are you going to do that?" Ward asked.

"I'll ask them to come. They're probably still in Toyah, and if they aren't, the sheriff there will more 'n likely know how to get ahold of them. So, I'll send a telegram to them through Sheriff, uh," Ty paused in mid-sentence to check the article in the paper, "through Sheriff Wallace. I'll have him give the telegram to Will or Gid Crockett."

"Ha. They're famous men, Ty. You may as well ask Wild Bill Hickock, or Wyatt Earp to come to Tilden."

"Wild Bill Hickock is dead, and I don't know Wyatt Earp. But I do know Will and Gid Crockett, they're friends of mine. And if I ask 'em, they'll come."

"Will and Gid Crockett are friends of yours?" Ward asked, surprised by the revelation.

"Longtime friends," Ty said.

"Why is it that you've never said anything about that?"

"I don't know, I guess it's because the subject has never come up before."

* * *

After witnessing the hanging, Martin Baker left Reeves County traveling in a casual eastern drift, until he wound up in Tom Greene County. He stopped in front of a country store near the town of Sherwood.

"Good afternoon, sir," the store clerk greeted Baker when he walked in. There were no other customers in the store.

"I need to do a little shopping," Baker said.

"Yes, sir," the store clerk replied with a broad smile. "That's what we're here for."

Baker began giving the store clerk his order: a slab of cured bacon, six cans of beans, six cans of peaches, a sack of ground coffee, a sack of flour and a sack of sugar.

"Oh, my, that's quite an order," the store clerk said as he placed the last item on the counter."

"Yeah, well, I'm travellin'," Baker said.

"Yes, sir. Let's see, that comes to . . ."

"Nothin'," Baker replied.

"I beg your pardon?"

"It comes to nothin'. I ain't payin' for it."

"Oh, now, look here, sir! You can't do that," the clerk

said, adamantly.

"Yeah, I can," Baker said, and pulling his pistol, he shot the clerk. Then, in addition to putting all his groceries in a cloth bag, he emptied the cash drawer.

"Eighty-seven dollars? That's all you've got?" Baker said, though as the clerk was dead, he was actually talking to himself.

Baker got a can of kerosine, sprinkled it on the wooden floor, then set a match to it. He rode away from the store with his grocery bag hanging from the saddle horn. Behind him the flames had taken hold, and now black smoke was climbing into the air.

Will and Gid were to receive a one-thousand-dollar reward from the state of Texas, plus an additional one thousand dollars from the Cattlemen's Association. They had stayed for the trial and the hanging, and now were remaining in Toyah long enough for the rewards to be paid.

When they saw Sheriff Wallace come into the saloon carrying something, they smiled in anticipation of receiving the reward.

"Here's the reward money," Sheriff Wallace said.

"Thank, you, thank you kindly," Will said, reaching for the two envelopes. But when he took the two white envelopes, there was a smaller, yellow envelope still in Sheriff Wallace's hand.

"Is there any reason you're carrying a telegram with you?"

"That depends," Sheriff Wallace said.

"Depends on what?"

"On whether or not you know a sheriff by the name of Ty McMurtry."

"Yes, we know him," Gid replied with an enthusiastic smile.

"We didn't know he was a sheriff though," Will added. "Is that telegram for us?"

"Actually it was for me, asking my help in locating you."

"From the expression on your face, I gather it isn't a telegram trying to arrange a revival among old friends."

"I suppose in a way, it is. But it's a little more than that."

"How in the world did Ty find us?" Gid asked.

"What you did for us made the newspapers all over the state. Sheriff McMurtry read the story and sent you this telegram, in hopes that I could get it to you."

Will took the telegram.

WILL GID READ OF YOUR EXPLOITS NEED HELP STOP CAN YOU COME TO TILDEN STOP YOUR OLD FRIEND SHERIFF TY MCMURTRY

"Well, Little Brother, it would appear that our old friend needs our help."

"I wonder what he needs help with," Gid asked.

"Does it matter? If he has asked us for help, you know

damn well we're going to be there for him," Will said.

"You'll get no argument from me, but do you think we can eat first?"

"I think we can make time to get a bite or two. Or in your case, a bite or fifty," Will replied with a little chuckle.

Looking at the map, the brothers decided that the closest they could get to Tilden by train, was Cotulla, in La Salle County. Because it would be an overnight trip, they bought tickets on a Pullman Sleeper car, then arranged for their horses to be transported in a stock car that was attached just for that purpose.

Before the train arrived, Will replied to Ty's telegram.

RECEIVED MESSAGE WILL ARRIVE TILDEN IN TWO DAYS STOP CROCKETTS

The train they were to catch came steaming into the station, and after making certain that their horses were loaded into the stock car, they boarded.

"I wonder what they'll be serving in the dining car," Gid said.

Will laughed.

"What are you laughing at? I'm serious."

"You asked that question as if you might actually refuse to eat, if it didn't meet your standards."

Gid chuckled as well. "Big brother, have you ever seen any food that didn't meet my standards?"

Boarding the train at one-thirty in the afternoon, the schedule called for them to reach Cotulla at two-fifteen the following afternoon.

During the long afternoon of the first day, they talked of the days when they and Ty were young boys, on neighboring farms.

"Do you remember when the three of us went dove hunting, and we took all the pellets out of Ty's shotgun shells?" Gid asked. "You and I were bringing down birds with just about every shot, and we kept teasing Ty for missing every bird he shot at."

"Yeah," Will said. "He got me back pretty good though, when I went skinny dipping and he took my clothes and hid them while you and he had a picnic with Katie, Jennie, and Edna. I had to stay in the water for over an hour while the five of you ate fried chicken. And you didn't leave me a single crumb. You'll never be able to convince me that you didn't have something to do with that."

"Well, I might have invited the girls," Gid admitted.

"And, ate my share of the chicken," Will added.

"Well, who can blame me, Will, it was damn good chicken. Besides, after that dirty trick you pulled on Ty, taking all the shot from his shell. What did you expect?"

"What do you mean, the dirty trick *I* pulled? We were both involved in that, as I recall."

"Yeah, well, somehow Ty got the idea that it was

only you."

"*Somehow*, he got that idea?"

"And the chicken was just really good, Big Brother. Too bad you didn't get any."

"Tell me now, why I put up with you?"

"Because I'm your favorite brother?"

Will laughed. "Well, since you are my only brother, I don't suppose I can argue with you about that."

* * *

Martin Baker was in the Watering Hole saloon in Kerrville, having come a little over three hundred miles from Toyah. He felt safe here, because he was certain there would be nobody who recognized him.

"Buy me another drink, honey?" the percentage girl asked.

"Stella, I ain't done nothin' but buy you drinks for the two days I've been here," Baker said.

"Oh, that ain't all you've done, honey," Stella said, rubbing her hand along her hip and smiling suggestively.

"Go away and let me read my newspaper," Baker said.

With a pout of rejection, Stella left Baker's table, and started out in search of another cowboy.

Baker wasn't interested in reading the entire newspaper, only the story that had caught his attention.

FELTON GANG STILL AT WORK

Residents of LaSalle, McMullen, Live Oak and Bee counties continue to suffer under the pillaging of Jess Felton and his gang. His most recent depredation was the robbery of the bank in Pettus. Not content with taking the money, Felton killed the bank teller, a woman customer, and her seven-year-old child.

Sheriffs Milton Andrews of La Salle county, Tyrone McMurtry of McMullen county, Andrew Webb of Live Oak county, and Edgar Till of Bee county have placed bringing Jess Felton to justice, as their number one priority, and have agreed to cooperate across county lines if need be.

Baker drummed his fingers on the folded newspaper and smiled. So, that's where Jess Felton wound up. The two had been neighbors with similar backgrounds, having lost their parents at an early age. Jess was raised by his uncle, Baker was also raised by an uncle. The two of them had been apprenticed to the same farm family. They ran away together, and for a while, were partners in crime until they decided to go their separate ways.

Baker put the paper down, and decided to try and look up his old friend, if he could find him. And it seemed to him that La Salle County might be a good place to start.

Ty was taking his supper in The Iron Skillet. His dining companion was Mike Jensen, editor of the *Tilden Free Press*.

"Felton and his gang are giving La Salle County hell," Jensen said.

"Yes, well it isn't only La Salle County, They've been pretty busy all over this part of the state," Ty said.

"That's the problem, bouncing around like that, you sheriffs can't leave your county unprotected while you go after them," Jensen said.

"I won't be going after them."

"Well, damn, Ty, I admit that I can see your point, but I hate to think of those sons of bitches getting away with murder without anyone even pursuing them," Jensen said.

Ty smiled. "I didn't say nobody would go after them. I said I wouldn't be going after them."

"Who will be going then?"

"I'd rather not say until they get here."

"They?"

"A couple of friends of mine."

"And you say they're coming here specifically to go after Felton?"

"Yes."

"Ty, you said they were a couple friends of yours. First, do they know what they'll be in for, and secondly, do you think they're the match for Felton?"

"I haven't told them yet, but believe me, these two are more than a match for Felton and his men."

Chapter Seven

Ty's deputy sheriff, Ward Haller, was sitting in a swing on Dr. Burke's front porch. His companion at the moment was Dr. Burke's very attractive daughter, Anna. Ward and Anna were, in the words of Miss Flossie Schaefer, the sixty-five year old spinster who kept track of such things, 'keeping company.'

"It was awful, what happened in Pettus," Anna said. "Folks are saying that it was the Jess Felton gang."

"It was," Ward agreed.

"I just wish someone could catch him."

"Don't worry, he and his whole gang will soon be caught, and punished," the deputy said.

"Oh, Ward, no!" Anna said, putting her hand on his shoulder. "I didn't mean for you to go after him. He has a whole gang, and I'd be afraid for you and for Sheriff McMurtry if I thought you would be going after him by yourselves."

"You don't have to worry. Neither one of us will be going after Jess Felton. But I know who will be, and believe me, they are formidable."

"Are they good men, or are they just bounty hunters?"

"It is possible, you know, to be both a good man, and a bounty hunter. In this case, even though they will be paid a bounty, I wouldn't particularly classify them as bounty hunters. They are really good friends of the sheriff, who happen also to be skilled man-hunters."

"Do you know them?"

"I know of them. "

"Who are they?"

"I think it might be best to keep their identity secret until they actually arrive, and agree to get involved."

Anna smiled broadly. "Oh, a secret! I love a secret."

As the train roared through the night, the two brothers flipped a coin for the berths. Gid won, and chose the upper. That left Will with the lower berth and though the beds were equally as comfortable, he was awakened by the depot activity of every town they passed through.

On one such occasion, Will didn't know what town they were in, or even what time it was, though he knew it was well into the middle of the night. He could see the activity on the depot platform, illuminated as it was by several gas lamps. One young woman hugged a young man goodbye, then stayed behind, crying as he boarded the train.

Because Will was lying in the dark, invisible to anyone outside the train, he couldn't help but feel that he was invading the privacy of the young woman. He looked away.

The two brothers slept through the rest of the night, then had breakfast shortly after the dining car opened.

"I wonder what Ty wants with us," Gid asked.

"I don't know, but knowing Ty, I don't believe he would ask for our help if he didn't need it."

Ty had been a sergeant under Will Crockett during the war, but even before that, the McMurtry farm was adjacent to the Crockett farm back in Missouri.

"Ty's a good man, so whatever he wants, I intend to do it, if it's at all possible," Will said.

"Or even if we don't think it's possible," Gid added.

"Yes, I don't intend to turn away, regardless of the job."

Because he had so often been awakened during the night, Will was napping when they finally rolled into the Cotulla depot.

"Wake up, Will," Gid said. "We're here."

"Cotulla," the conductor said, walking through the car. "Folks, this is Cotulla, Texas."

"Conductor, we'll need to get our horses off here," Will said.

60

"Yes, sir, we'll have plenty of time for that," the conductor said.

The sun was high and hot when they stepped down from the train. Nobody else got off the train, and though there were a few people standing out on the platform, they were apparently here only as gawkers. None of them showed any sign of boarding the train, and Will and Gid were the only passengers who left the train.

While they waited for their horses to be off loaded, Will and Gid retrieved their saddles from the baggage car, their personal luggage being only what could be carried in the saddle bags.

"It will be interesting to see if Ty has changed much since we last saw him," Will said.

"I wonder if he's heard from Katie?"

Katie was Ty's sister, and just before the war broke out, Katie and Gid had fallen in love. Everyone knew that they were going to be married, but the war changed all that. A little over a year ago, Gid and Katie had met up again, but by then, Katie was calling herself Cat. Katie, as Cat, had taken up "the oldest profession" believing that was the only way she could survive. It had been a bittersweet meeting, the old feeling between them was still there and Gid was willing to accept Katie for what she was. But Katie was too shamed by what she had become, so there was no reconciliation.

It would be an overnight ride to Tilden, and when they made camp that evening, they opened a can of beans, warmed them, and fried a few pieces of cured ham on the fire they built.

"The beans and ham are pretty good," Gid said. "But not as good as the oysters we had in the dining car last night."

"I'm amazed you would say that, Little Brother," Will teased.

"Why are you amazed? Didn't you think they were good?"

"Yes, I thought they were very good, but I didn't know you actually tasted food, I thought you just ate."

"Har, de, har har," Gid said. "You are so funny," he added, sarcastically.

Some two hundred miles behind Will and Gid, but headed in the same direction was Martin Baker. He had run out of beans and peaches, so he was having a supper of fried bacon. He was heading for Pettus. He knew there was no way that Felton would actually still be in the same town where he had robbed a bank, but Baker had to start looking for him somewhere, and this was his last known location.

Baker knew that Felton had been in Pettus at least one time, and the reason he knew, was because Baker had been with him. The two were still in their boyhood when they held up a liquor store in Pettus.

Baker chuckled as he remembered it. They had gotten fifty-eight dollars, which seemed like a fortune to them, then.

As Baker recalled holding up the liquor store he remembered, that in addition to the money, they also got two bottles of whiskey. The thought reminded him that he had drunk the last of his whiskey, two days ago. He planned to visit a saloon in the next town he came to, and he would buy another bottle of whiskey to take with him.

And a few more cans of peaches.

It was mid-afternoon of the next day when Will and Gid rode into the town of Tilden.

TILDEN

Pop 851

County Seat of

McMullen County

They entered the town on Center Street, flanked by businesses on both sides. The first business they rode by was the Tilden Apothecary, then Hart's Bakery, then the Clark and Hopkins Freight Haulers. There were three wagons backed up to the loading dock at Clark and Hopkins, one was being loaded, the other two were being unloaded. Next to Clark and Hopkins, they saw the stagecoach depot. An empty coach was standing in front of the depot, as the hostler was connecting the team. At the corner of Center and Second Street they saw Beck's Livery, and dismounting stepped inside. There, they saw a gray-haired man examining pieces of a clock that he had spread out on the counter before him. He looked up as they entered.

"You here to board your horses?" the gray-haired man asked.

"No, I want my clock fixed," Gid said.

The man got a confused look on his face, then, with a laugh he swept his hand over the clock parts display before him.

"Yes, sir, yes, sir, that's a good one," he said. "This blasted clock quit on me, and I thought I might be able to get it running again, but I'm afraid I've bitten off more than I can chew. Now, what can I do for you?"

"You can board our horses for us," Will said.

"Yes, sir, that'll be a dollar a day, oats and rubdown."

"You'll store our tack?"

"That I will."

"We'll be back for our saddle bags when we're checked into the hotel. And, could you tell us where the sheriff's office is?"

"That's easy, it's down at the far end of the block, on

the opposite side of the street."

Will pulled out a twenty-dollar bill. "You are Mr. Beck, are you?"

"I am."

"I'm Will Crockett, this is my brother Gid. This will cover ten days for the two of us. If we're here longer, I'll drop back by."

"Very good, sir, I'll get them all taken care of," Beck replied.

After they boarded their horses, Will and Gid walked down to the sheriff's office. Stepping inside, they saw Ty McMurtry, now wearing a sheriff's star. With a huge grin he stood up, and then came to greet the two brothers with his hand extended.

"Will, Gid," he said. "It's great to see you. It's been years. Thank you for coming."

"We're just lucky your telegram caught us," Will said. "We do move around quite a bit."

"Ah, yes, but your . . . exploits, shall we call them, are so often printed in the newspapers that I've been able to keep track of you. Then, of course, I read about that nasty business out in Toyah."

"Well, I'm glad you were able to find us," Will said.

There was another man in the office, younger than Sheriff McMurtry, wearing the star of a Deputy Sheriff.

"Oh," Sheriff McMurtry said. "Let me introduce you to my deputy, as fine a young man as you'll ever hope to meet. Will, Gid Crockett, this is Ward Haller. Ward, you've heard me speak of these two men. The Crockett Brothers have become famous, but I'm happy to say I knew them long before that. We grew up together as neighbors."

"And he was the big brother to the prettiest girl in the whole state of Missouri," Gid said. "Tell me, Ty, what have you heard from Katie?"

The smile left Ty's face to be replaced by an expression of sorrow. "You mean you haven't heard?"

"Haven't heard what?"

"She died of childbirth fever after having a baby. Her husband was all broken up over it, but he's been just real good with the baby."

"I . . . I didn't know that," Gid said, feeling a great sense of loss. "When did it happen?"

"It's been over six months now. I'm sorry to be the one to have to tell you, I seem to recall that there was something between you and my sister. But that was all so long ago that I'd nearly forgotten about it."

"I'm glad she found a good man," Gid said.

"She did, he treated her well, and like I said, he's been real good with the baby. A little boy."

"Ty, you said you needed help," Will said, changing the subject from the melancholy.

"Yes. I've got you boys a couple of rooms at the Morning Star Hotel. Why don't you get settled in, have supper with me at The Iron Skillet tonight, and I'll fill you in on what's going on."

"You're buying us supper?" Gid asked.

"Well, McMullen County is," Sheriff McMurtry replied. He smiled. "I remember what kind of appetite you have, so I'm not sure I could afford to feed you, on a sheriff's salary."

"Womenfolk are always telling me that they like a man with a good appetite," Gid replied.

"Then why is it that Will is more popular with the ladies than you are?" Sheriff McMurtry teased.

"Oh, you do know how to hurt a man," Gid said with an exaggerated wince.

Will laughed. "It looks like he got you there, Little Brother. So, tell me, Ty, I've been so out of touch with you, that I don't know what's going on in your life. Are you married?"

Ty chuckled. "I'm not married, but I am keeping company with a fine woman."

"What about you, Deputy? Are you married?" Will asked.

"Not yet, but I've got plans. That is, if the young lady will have me."

"Oh, I don't think there's any doubt but that Anna

would have you," Ty said. "It's her papa you might have to worry about."

"Gid, what do you say we get checked in to the hotel, then get us a beer?" Will suggested.

"If you're going to a saloon, I recommend The Tinderbox," Sheriff McMurtry said. "Clyde Tilghman is the bartender there. Tell him that I sent you."

"He'll give us a better deal that way?" Will asked.

McMurtry chuckled. "No, you won't be getting any better deal, but I'll get a free beer for sending you there."

Chapter Eight

"So, that's the Crockett brothers you've been telling me about," Deputy Haller said after the two left.

"That's them," Sheriff McMurtry replied.

"I wouldn't want to make that big one mad," Haller said. "I plan to stay on his good side."

"That would probably be a pretty good idea," the sheriff agreed with a little chuckle.

Haller took his hat down from the peg, and put it on. "It's about time I took a walk around town to check up on things."

"Yeah, you are a few minutes late for your afternoon rounds. I'm sure all the young single women in town are getting a little anxious now, because they haven't seen you."

Ward Haller was fifteen years younger than Ty McMurtry, and a very good-looking man. Ty McMurtry's comment was based upon the fact that so many young women in town were taken with him.

But there was only one woman in town who held Ward's interest. The problem was that Anna Burke was the daughter of the doctor, an educated man. And though Ward was comfortable with the idea that Anna returned his feelings, he didn't know what her father would think about her taking up with a deputy sheriff.

Jess Felton was sitting on a rock eating an apple. When he finished, he tossed the core away then started back toward the small, isolated cabin that he used for the headquarters of his gang. Right now, counting himself, his gang numbered four: Julius Paxton, Edgar Kildeer, and Paddy O'Neal.

They had taken just under eleven hundred dollars from the Bank of Pettus and dividing it meant $180.00 for each of his men, and $360.00 for Felton who, because he was the leader of the gang, took two shares.

The other members of his gang were getting a little antsy by now. They had joined up with Felton because they were convinced that he could get them high-paying jobs. One hundred and eighty dollars was six months' salary as a cow-hand, something all of them had done. But they all had aspirations for something much more lucrative.

Earlier today, Felton told them that he had plans

for them, big plans, that would pay off within another couple of days.

Felton held up a copy of a newspaper, and smiling, let the others in on his plan.

"According to this newspaper, the Bank of Tilden is sending fifteen thousand dollars to the bank in Fowler Town. I've got an idea that it's not going to make it there, because we're goin' to take it."

"Damn right!"

"Why do you think they would put something like that in the newspaper?" Kildeer asked.

"What difference does it make?" Felton asked. "The money will be on the coach, we'll be there to take it."

"It's just that I don't have a very good feeling about this," Kildeer insisted.

"All right, stay here if you don't want to come with us. That'll just mean more money for the rest of us."

"No, no, now, don't get me wrong. I intend to go, and I intend to get my fair share. I'm just saying that there seems to be something a little strange about this is all."

Fifteen minutes after taking their rooms at the Morning Star Hotel, Will and Gid pushed through the bat-wing doors and stepped into The Tinderbox Saloon. As was their custom, Gid moved to one side of the door and Will to the other. Pressing their backs against the front wall, they studied the shadowed interior. There were three men standing at the bar, four men at one of the tables, and three more at another. The remaining tables were empty. There were two women in the saloon, one visiting with the men who were standing at the bar, and the other sitting at a table with the three men.

Both women, wearing scandalously low-cut dresses abandoned the men they were with, and came to greet Will and Gid, doing so with the practiced smiles of their profession. And though both women showed some of the wear of their profession, they were still attractive enough to gain the attention of the men customers.

"Hello boys," one of them said. "I'm Fancy, this is Rebel. How would you like to have a couple of drinks with us?"

"Sounds like a pretty good idea to me," Gid replied. "What do you say Big Brother. Shall we buy these two young ladies a drink?"

"You call him big brother?" Fancy asked.

"He's older 'n me," Gid said as if that explained it. "But I'm a lot better looking." He put his hand on Fancy's arm and escorted her up to the bar.

"My brother and I will have a beer," Will said, "and these two young ladies will have whatever they want. Are you Clyde Tilghman?" he asked the bartender.

"Yes, but how do you know?"

"Sheriff McMurtry told us, and he also said to tell you

72

that he sent us here."

Clyde chuckled. "It's been a month o' Sundays since Ty McMurtry paid for his own beer. He set the drinks before Will, Gid, and the two women."

"Here's to you," Gid said, raising his beer in salute to Fancy.

"Hey, Fancy, what are you doin' with them two?" someone called. He was sitting with two other men at the table Fancy had just abandoned. "You're supposed to be entertaining us. We didn't tell you that you could be with anyone else."

"I'm a working girl, Doodle, I have to make a living," Fancy replied. "You 'n Harry, 'n Jaco ain't bought me no new drinks 'n near-bout an hour now."

"You get your ass back over here 'n leave them two alone."

Fancy turned back toward Gid. "Never mind them," she said.

The one called Doodle stepped up to the bar and, without warning, slapped Fancy.

Gid, reacting quickly, knocked Doodle down. Doodle's two friends jumped up from the table and charged toward Gid. One of them even got a blow in before Gid reacted, and the fight turned quickly into an outright brawl between Gid and the three men.

Will turned around to lean his back against the bar,

drinking his beer, and just casually enjoying the fight.

"Aren't you going to help him?" Fancy asked. She was still holding her hand against her cheek, but she was clearly concerned that the three big men might hurt Gid. "That's your brother."

"I'm trying to keep the fight fair," Will said.

"Fair? What do you mean? There's three of them."

"That's what I mean, there are only three of them. Why should I stop Gid's fun?"

"You mean..." Fancy started to say but was interrupted when she saw Doodle crash into the table, turning it over.

By now the others in the bar were adding to the excitement, cheering Gid, Doodle, Harry, and Jaco on. The noise of the fight began bringing people in off the street.

Will continued to lean back against the bar, drinking his beer and looking on, casually. He saw the biggest of Gid's three adversaries crash to the floor.

"Oh, good one, Little Brother," Will congratulated.

The remaining man, still on his feet, looked at the two, who were slow getting up from the floor, showing no interest in continuing the fight.

"No, no more," the remaining man said, holding his hands out in front of him, palm forward.

"All right, all right, break it up in here!" Sheriff McMurtry called, rushing into the saloon then in response to the disturbance. "Who started this?"

"That big son of a bitch started it," one of the men Gid had been fighting said. "Without so much as a fare-the-well, he just knocked Doodle down. So me'n Jaco decided to teach him a lesson."

"Ha! Some lesson," Sheriff McMurtry said. "It makes you wonder who was the teacher 'n who was the student."

"It wasn't started for nothin', Ty," the bartender said. "This big feller was doin' no more 'n just talkin' with Fancy, when Doodle come up here 'n slapped her. He knocked Doodle down, then Harry 'n Jaco commenced to jumpin' on him."

Ty McMurtry chuckled, then nodded. "Folks," he said to the others. "Let me introduce these two fellas to you." He pointed to Will. "This is Will Crockett, 'n the big man there, is his brother Gid. They are a couple of old friends of mine, 'n I asked them to come to Tilden to help me out. And you're lucky you didn't get him mad; I once saw him take on five men at the same time. Now, you three come with me. I think you need to spend the night in jail to cool off."

"Now, look here, you ain't got no call to be puttin' us in jail," Harry said.

"I'm doin' it for your own good," McMurtry said. "I'm afraid you might try and do with a gun, what you couldn't do with your fists, and that might involve the other brother. If you try 'n come after either one of these boys with a gun, you'll be dead before your body hits the floor."

At supper time Will and Gid walked down to The Iron Skillet Restaurant.

"I wonder what Ty wants with us," Gid asked.

"I don't know, but we're soon going to find out. There he is," Gid said, pointing to a table in the back corner of the room.

Sheriff McMurtry looked up as Will and Gid approached his table. "No more fights?" he asked with a smile.

"I'm willing to give odds, but so far no takers," Will teased.

"No, and it's getting damn boring," Gid said.

Ty chuckled. "Have a seat," he offered.

"What's the special today?" Gid asked.

"What difference does it make, you'll eat it," Will said.

"Well, yeah, but I eat some things with more gusto than other things."

"What about chicken and dumplings?"

"Yeah, now that I can eat with particular gusto."

As they were finishing their meal, Sheriff McMurtry told them why he had invited them.

"Have you ever heard of a man by the name of Jess Felton?"

Will and Gid exchanged a quick glance, then Will answered for them. "I don't think we have."

"Well, to be honest, I'm not even sure that's his real name," Sheriff McMurtry said. "But Felton has a gang that has been terrorizing all of a four county area. It came to a head a couple of weeks ago when Felton and his men robbed a bank in Pettus. During the robbery they killed the teller, a woman customer and her seven-year-old son."

"How do you know it was Felton?" Gid asked.

"There were enough townspeople who heard the shooting and saw them leave the bank. At least three of them recognized him."

"That's convincing enough," Will said.

"By the way, there is a five-hundred-dollar reward that's been offered for Felton, and I think there's at least a two hundred and fifty-dollar reward for any of his men. So, not only will you be doing me a favor, you'll be making a little money for yourselves."

"Is there any way we can talk to any of the witnesses who identified them?" Will asked.

"Well Dan is the only one who saw it, who actually lives here. He was in Pettus delivering a wagon when it happened. As it turns out, he also knows Felton."

"How does he know him?"

"I think I should let Dan tell you. Come on down to the office after you have breakfast tomorrow morning, and I'll have Ward take you to see him."

Chapter Nine

Dr. Milton Burke was the only doctor in Tilden so had an expanded facility, a doctor's office where he saw patients on an out-patient basis, an operating room, and four recovery rooms. His living quarters were above his office. He had been an army surgeon during the war, then after that, he had moved here with his wife and daughter to set up a practice. Minnie had been his nurse and they had planned to grow old together and enjoy the grandchildren when they came. Sadly, Minnie had died six years earlier, and now there was only his daughter, Anna, to share his living quarters.

When Dr. Burke came up from his office that evening, he was greeted by the smell of fried pork chops.

"Do I smell what I think I smell?" he called out.

"I don't know, what do you think you smell?" Anna said, by way of greeting him. "Hello, Papa, did you have a busy day?"

"Mrs. Sidwell was in complaining of the gout. I sure wish I could do something for her. I've tried just about every nostrum I know but she doesn't seem to be getting any better."

"Mrs. Sidwell is a widow, isn't she?" Anna asked.

"Yes, Ted has been dead some two years now."

Anna smiled. "And mama has been dead for six years."

"What are you trying to say, girl?"

"Don't you think it just might be that Henrietta Sidwell has set her cap for you?"

"Humph. Well, if she has, she's sure lowered her target. There are a lot of men who are better looking than I am."

"Papa, a woman would rather have a good man, than a good-looking man."

"Ha! And what do you know about what a woman wants?"

"Papa, surely it can't have escaped your sight that I'm no longer your little girl. I'm a woman now."

"Lord, darlin', don't I know it. You could get married any day now, and I'd wind up all alone."

Anna kissed her father on the cheek. "If he won't take you, he can't have me."

"How long before supper?"

"It's ready now, and Ward should be here any minute."

"Ward? Wait a minute, are you telling me that the

deputy sheriff is going to have supper with us? How many times does that make this week that he's eaten with us? Are we taking him to raise?"

Anna laughed. "You like Ward, you know you do."

"I do like the boy. And I'd rather he be seeing you under my nose, than behind my back. But if he keeps on eating here, I'm going to have to get a menu from The Iron Skillet and start charging Ward for his meals."

"Papa, you wouldn't do a thing like that, would you?" Anna asked, aghast.

"Well, it's just a thought," Dr. Burke said with a little laugh. At almost that same moment, there was a knock at the door.

"I'll get it, it must be Ward," Anna said.

The apartment could be reached through the doctor's office, and via the outdoor stairs that climbed up the side of the building. Ward had come up the outdoor stairs and was standing on the landing when Anna opened the door.

"Oh good, you're on time. Come on in, supper's almost ready, and Papa is in the parlor.

"Hello, Ward," Dr. Burke greeted when Anna brought him into the parlor.

"Hello, Doc," Ward replied. "Oh and thank you for inviting me to supper."

"Supper? You mean you're here for supper?" Dr. Burke got a surprised look on his face.

"Papa!" Anna said sharply.

Dr. Burke looked at his daughter and smiled, before he responded. "I was teasing you, Ward, of course I knew you were coming for supper, and we're always glad to have you. By the way, you are a young man who always has his fingers on the pulse of our community. Anything new going on?"

"Yes sir, Ty sent for some old friends of his to come help us out with Felton and his bunch. The Crocketts."

"Who?" Anna asked.

"The Crockett Brothers, Will and Gid." Ward replied. "I can't believe you've never heard of them. Their names are in the newspapers all the time, and there have even been a couple of books written about 'em."

"Books written about them?"

"Sort of."

"Sort of? Then I take it they aren't exactly biographies," Dr. Burke said.

"Actually, they're penny dreadfuls, but the stories are exciting because Will and Gid are exciting people."

Anna Burke smiled, prettily. "Why, Ward Haller, you sound positively excited about meeting them."

"Well, I wouldn't say I'm excited, or anything like that," Ward said. "But they *are* famous people. And they seem like a couple of straight shooters."

"I've heard of them," Dr. Burke said. "And I must say

that I'm surprised that Ty would bring them here. From all that I have heard of the Crockett brothers, they are right on the edge of being outlaws themselves."

"They're good men," Ward insisted. "Ty has told me all about them. Like I say, he and they are old friends. They grew up together."

"Papa, they have to be better than Jess Felton. And if they get rid of Felton and his men, that would be a good thing, wouldn't it?"

"Well, I must confess that I've never heard anything really bad about them. And from all I've read, they've never killed anyone who didn't need killing. Though, the whole concept of someone 'needing' killing, doesn't sit well with me. Perhaps it is my interpretation of the Hippocratic Oath."

"It's about time to eat," Anna said.

"Good, that smells like fried porkchops, and it's making me really hungry," Ward said.

"Young man, one of these days I'm going to want to know what your intentions are for my daughter?"

"Papa!" Anna squealed, her cheeks burning in embarrassment.

Dr. Burke laughed. "Pay no attention to my prattle. I was just teasing you, son."

"You're quite the jokester tonight," Anna said, ameliorating her charge with a smile.

"You're always welcome at our table, Ward," Dr. Burke said.

"Thank you, Doctor, I appreciate that," Ward replied.

* * *

Anna waited until after Ward had left, before she mentioned the letter. "I got a letter from Aunt Mildred today. She wants me to come to Fowler Town and spend a few days with her."

"Is anything wrong?"

"No, it's just that her birthday is coming up, and I think she doesn't want to be alone."

"Her birthday. Oh, my, my only sister and I just completely forgot about her birthday. Yes, of course you can go. I'll buy a present for you to take."

Anna chuckled. "You already have. You bought her a hat."

"Oh I did, did I? Looking out for me, were you?"

"Papa, you are the only doctor in town," Anna said. "You don't have time to go shopping. And I didn't mind doing it for you."

"When will you be leaving?"

"I've got a ticket on the stage coach, leaving at ten o'clock tomorrow morning."

"Well, have a good time with your visit, but don't stay

too long. In addition to being my nurse, I'll actually miss you around here."

"Indeed. Well, it's glad to know that I'm wanted. And anyway, I'll be back before you know it."

"You'll be hurrying back for me, or for Ward?" Dr. Burke asked.

"Why Papa. For you of course," Anna said. Then a broad smile spread across her face. "And for Ward."

* * *

The town of Frio City wasn't that large, but it was the first settlement that Martin Baker had ridden through in several days. He still had enough money remaining from his holdup of the little general store in Tom Green County almost two weeks earlier, to buy his supper, a few drinks, and even to stay in a hotel tonight.

At first Baker had planned to take his supper in a restaurant, then get a few drinks, but as he rode down the dark street of the town, the saloon seemed the most inviting. Tying his horse off out front, he pushed through the swinging doors and stepped up to the bar.

"What'll it be?" the bartender asked.

"Can I get supper here?"

"Yes, sir, you sure can. Fried ham, taters 'n onions."

"All right," Baker said. "And a beer. I'll be over there."

He pointed to an empty table.

There was a card game going on at the table next to the one Baker took. One of the players gave out a happy explanation while the other three groaned.

"Damn, Cedric, you've won four out of the last five hands," someone said. "You must be more'n a hunnert dollars up, by now."

"Let's just say this," Cedric replied. "If the baby needed new shoes, and if I had a baby, I could sure as hell afford to buy 'em."

Baker's meal and beer were brought to his table, and as he ate, he listened to the conversation at the adjacent table.

"All right, Cedric, beat three jacks," one of the players said after the next hand was played.

"I think a ten high full house will do just that," Cedric said to the groans of the other players.

Just as Baker finished his supper, he heard a declaration for Cedric. "I think I'll head back to the ranch."

"What the hell, Cedric, you're not going to quit while you're ahead, are you?" one of the other players asked.

"Of course, I'm going to quit while I'm ahead. That's the whole purpose of playing cards, isn't it? Why would you keep playing until you were behind?"

"It just doesn't seem like the sportin' thing to do, is all."

"All right, one more hand," Cedric said. "One more hand, and then I'm leaving."

"You'll be staying in town tonight, will you? You sure have enough money to get you a hotel room."

"Now why would I pay for a hotel room, when just two miles north of here there's a bunkhouse that's free?" Cedric replied. "Whose deal is it?"

Baker stepped up to the bar. "What's the hotel like in this town?" he asked.

"It's clean, not too expensive," the bartender said.

"I've been sleeping on the ground for weeks, I'm looking forward to spending the night in bed," Baker said.

Leaving the saloon, Baker rode down to the hotel, tied his horse up behind the hotel, then walked around to come in through the front door.

"I haven't slept in a couple of days, so I don't want to be disturbed tonight," he said as he signed the hotel registration book. "But I would like for someone to wake me up by around seven in the morning."

"Yes sir, Mister uh," the clerk checked the signature, "Morris."

Taking his key, Baker went up the front stairway, then hurried to the back of the corridor and came down the back stairs, being careful to not be seen. Then, mounting his horse he rode north down the alley until he was out of town. He rode about a mile down the road, then he waited.

He didn't have to wait more than about fifteen minutes until he saw a rider coming toward him. Because of the twilight and the distance, Baker couldn't be certain that this was the card player, but he reasoned that it had to be him.

He started riding back toward town in an unhurried gait that aroused no attention. As the distance was closed between them, he was able to identify the rider as Cedric, the card player.

"Good evening, sir," Cedric said, touching the brim of his hat with his fingers.

Baker already had his pistol in his hand, and he raised it and pulled the trigger.

"What?" Cedric gasped, then he fell from his horse.

Baker dismounted and shot Cedric one more time, this time in the head. Searching his pockets, he found no money and was frustrated, then he thought of the saddlebags.

Cedric's horse had not moved since the shooting, and a quick search of the saddlebags proved fruitful.

"Yes!" Baker said aloud, as he pulled out a wad of bills.

Returning to town, Baker used the back stairs of the hotel to gain entrance to his hotel room. Once in his room, and with the lantern providing enough light for the task, he counted the money he had taken from Cedric. It came to one hundred and seventy-six dollars.

"Mr. Morris? Mr. Morris, sir?"

A banging on the door accompanied the call and for just a second, Baker wondered who Morris was. Then he remembered that he had registered as Morris.

"Yes?" he replied.

"Mr. Morris, it is seven o'clock, sir. You wished to be awakened."

"Yes, thank you," Baker said.

Fifteen minutes later, Baker was in the hotel dining room for breakfast. There seemed to be some agitation among the diners and hotel staff.

"What is it?" Baker asked the waiter. "What's going on?"

"Oh, such a tragic thing, sir," the waiter replied. "There was a murder last night."

"A murder? Where? Here in the Hotel?"

"No sir, on the road north of town."

"You don't say. Hmm, I wonder why I didn't hear anything about it?"

"Oh, I don't see how you could have, sir. You checked in at seven o'clock last night. You were, most likely, already in bed."

"Yes, I was," Baker said. "A murder, huh? What a terrible thing."

Chapter Ten

Even before breakfast the next morning, Will and Gid walked down to the Sheriff's office to remind Ty that this morning they were to talk to the man who knew Jess Felton, and who had witnessed the bank robbery in Pettus.

"Yes, of course," Ty replied. "Ward, would you take Will and Gid down to Clark and Hopkins so they can talk to Dan Evans?"

"Sure, I'll take them," Ward said. "Come along, it's only a couple of blocks from here."

When they reached Clark and Hopkins' Wagon Freight yard, they found Evans sitting on the ground by a wagon wheel, packing the hub with grease.

"Dan, these two men are acting as special deputies, and they'll be looking for the men that robbed the bank in Pettus. They would like to talk to you."

"Can you talk to me while I'm workin'?" Evans asked. "I promised Mr. Clark that I'd have this wagon ready to roll out before dinner, 'n I'm already runnin' a little behind on it."

"That would be fine," Will said. "I've never been one for causing a man to interrupt his work."

"All right, what do you want to ask me?"

"Tell us what you saw."

"I'd drove one of the replacement wagons over to the Pettus warehouse of Clark and Hopkins. It's just across the street from the bank, 'n when I heard the shootin', I knowed right off what was happenin'. Three men, holdin' guns, come a runnin' outta the bank."

"Sheriff McMurtry said you saw Felton leaving the bank."

"That's right"

"How do you know it was Felton?"

Evans looked at Will, then at Deputy Haller. "Deputy, you mean neither you nor Sheriff McMurtry told 'em?"

"I imagine the sheriff wanted you to tell them," Haller said.

"The truth is, I took Jess in when he was no more 'n twelve years old. He was my sister's boy, 'n when the fever took her, 'n seein' as his pa was in prison, Jess had no place to go, so he come to live with me. He caused me nothin' but trouble from the very first day he come, 'n he finally run off when he was sixteen. I was so glad to see him go, that I didn't bother to go lookin' for 'im, and it's pretty obvious that I didn't do that good of a job at raisin' 'im."

"I don't suppose you would have any idea where we might find him, do you?"

"No, sir, I don't have no idea at all. Once the son of a bitch went bad on me, I didn't want nothin' else to do with 'im."

"Could you give us a good description so that we might recognize him if we see him?" Will asked.

"He ain't quite as tall as you are, 'n he don't weigh as much neither, but he ain't what you would call a little man. I'd say he's about average size. His face is pock marked from the smallpox he had when he was real young. 'N since he left my care, he's picked up a scar that's left 'im with a drooping left eye lid."

"What about the men who were with him? Did you recognize any of them?"

"No, I didn't, but to tell the truth, I didn't get all that good of a look at 'em. Soon as I seen Jess, I didn't really pay no attention to the rest of 'em. Then, when I come back here to Tilden, well, sir, I went right straight to the sheriff's office, 'n told him what I seen.

"I figured he'd more 'n likely be sendin' someone to talk to me."

"Thank you, Mr. Evans, you've been a big help," Will said.

"Jess's ma, my sister was a good woman. Mayhaps if she had lived, Jess would have turned out different, even iffen his pa was in prison. Mo Felton was about the sorriest son of a bitch that ever drew a breath. He's still in prison, and far as I'm concerned, they should 'a hung 'im a long time ago. But as it's turned out Jess's got too much of his pa's blood in 'im. I done the best I could with 'im, but I warn't married, so there warn't no woman aroun' to somewhat gentle him down none."

Dan watched Will and Gid leave the wagon yard, and he recalled the incident that had been the last straw between him, and his nephew. Jess had taken Mrs. Piercie's wash down from the line and burned every item of clothing the old lady had.

"Jess, why in the world would you do such a thing?" Dan asked.

"Ha! Did you see the way that old woman went jumpin' around in her back yard, screaming, 'n wringin' her hands? That's the funniest damn thing I ever seen."

"You will get a job, and you will pay Willena Piercie for every stitch of clothing you burned up."

"The hell I will," Jess Felton replied. Jess left that day, and never came back.

Dan had no idea how many men his nephew had killed, and though common sense told him that he wasn't responsible for any of them, he couldn't help but feel that he bore some of the blame.

After leaving the wagon yard, Will and Gid went to The Iron Skillet for breakfast when Sheriff McMurtry came to join them. He was carrying a newspaper.

"Come to buy us another meal, did you, Ty?" Gid asked.

"With the money you boys are going to make, you should be buying me meals," Ty said. "Ward said he thought your visit with Dan was productive."

"Yes, he described Felton for us, which will be a big help."

"Yes, but only if you can find him."

"Well, that's what we've set out to do," Will replied.

"I have an idea that might help."

"We'll take any help we can get," Will said.

"It has been reported in the paper that the bank here, is making a fifteen-thousand-dollar transfer to the bank in Fowler Town. The article says it'll be going out on the morning stage. If you two would . . ."

"Go on the stage as a decoy," Will said, finishing the sheriff's comment.

"Yes, exactly. I think the chances are pretty good that Felton will hit that stage. If he thinks there's a fifteen-thousand-dollar shipment, he won't pass up the opportunity."

"If he knows about it," Will said.

Sheriff McMurtry smiled then unfolded a copy of the newspaper and pointed to the front page. "This issue came out last week, so it's more than likely that Felton has already seen it."

LARGE MONEY SHIPMENT
TO FOWLER TOWN

Jay Montgomery announced yesterday that next week, Wednesday, October 9th, the amount of fifteen thousand dollars will be transferred via stagecoach from the Bank of Tilden to the Bank of Fowler Town. The shipment is being made in order to spread out the assets of the bank, and thus lessen the risk of having too much money on hand.

"Why would the bank make an announcement like that? That's just asking for. . ." Will started to ask, then, when he saw Ty smiling, he stopped in mid-sentence. "Wait a minute, that's exactly what you want, isn't it? You put this in the paper."

"Yes. I had it put it in the paper last week, as soon as I

heard that you would be here."

"What I don't understand is, how you got Montgomery to put his money up for bait like that."

"Easy. There is no money being shipped. I did let him know what I was doing, and there will be a locked bank bag delivered to the coach, but only Montgomery and I, and now you two, know that there's nothing in the bag. The newspaper editor doesn't know, and neither will the driver or the shotgun messenger know that it's a phony shipment. Hell, Ward doesn't even know that it's a phony shipment."

"If anything is going to draw Felton and his gang out, that damn sure should do it."

"Well, that's the plan," Ty said. He chuckled. "Ward thinks it was foolish of the bank to make the announcement. And of course, it would be, if it was real. But like I said, not even Ward knows it isn't real."

"Ward seems like a pretty nice fella," Gid said.

"He's as good as they come. I couldn't care anymore for him if he was my own son."

"Why didn't you let him know about the phony shipment?" Will asked.

"No specific reason, other than the fewer who know, the less likely Felton is to find out.

Will nodded. "Yes, I'd say you have a point there."

Felton, and the others of his gang had spent the night, not in the cabin that was their hideout, but camped alongside the road the coach would be taking.

"Boys, we ain't too far away from havin' more money 'n most of us has ever even seen," Felton said.

"Yeah, well, after this, you can get somebody else to take my place," Paddy O'Neal said.

"What do you mean? Why would we want to get someone else to take your place?" Kildeer asked.

"On account of I'm takin' my money to California. It don't never get cold there, 'n it don't cost almost nothin' to live there. Hell, I can prob'ly live the rest of my life on just my share."

"There ain't goin' to be no share at all, if there don't ever' body do their job," Felton said.

"What time you reckon the coach will get here?" Paxton asked.

"It's leavin' at ten o'clock, it'll prob'ly take about an hour to get this far."

Kildeer smiled. "Which means we'll all be rich by eleven o'clock."

"Kildeer, get up on that rock 'n keep your eyes open," Felton ordered. "The last thing we need is for somebody to come ridin' by, 'n seein' us here. I'll put someone else up there to replace you in another hour."

At about a quarter 'til ten, Will and Gid were standing in front of the stage depot, waiting for the bank messenger and Deputy Haller to deliver the sealed bank bag. They saw a very pretty young woman step down from a buggy that drove up.

"Thanks for the ride, Mr. Miller," the woman said.

"Glad to do it, Miss Burke," the middle-aged driver replied.

As the buggy drove off, she came toward the depot platform with a valise in hand.

"Excuse me, Miss," Will said. "Are you planning on taking the coach this morning?"

"Yes, sir, I'm going to visit my aunt in Fowler Town. Why do you ask?"

"It might be a good idea to pass on this coach and take the next one."

"That won't be until tomorrow, and my aunt's birthday is tomorrow. I don't want to miss half a day of her birthday because I'm on the road. Why do you suggest I not take this coach, anyway?"

"This coach will be taking a rather sizeable money shipment, and it might not be safe."

"Yes, I saw the announcement in the newspaper last week, and I thought it rather odd that they would make such a thing public. It seems to me like an announcement like that is just inviting the coach to be robbed."

Will didn't respond.

"Oh, my, that's exactly what it's supposed to do, isn't it?"

"You're a pretty astute woman, Miss . . . uh, I don't know your name."

"I see no reason why you should, but my name is Anna Burke. I take it you two will be on the coach?"

"Yes, ma'am, we will be."

"Protecting the money?"

"Well, uh, yes, we will be," Will replied.

Anna smiled, broadly. "Well, that settles it then, doesn't it? With you two protecting the money, it means you will also be protecting me. I'll be in no danger."

"I wish I could talk you out of it, but if you've already bought a ticket, I suppose you have every right to go with us," Will said.

A few minutes later a bank employee, carrying a locked, canvas pouch and accompanied by Deputy Haller, approached the waiting stagecoach.

"Here's the money shipment, Mr. Taylor," Deputy Haller said to the shotgun messenger as the bank employee passed the pouch up to him.

"Hello, Mr. Brandon," Anna said, greeting the bank employee. "Hello, Ward."

"Hello, Anna. Why are you here?" Ward asked. "Wait a minute, you aren't taking the stagecoach, are you?"

"I'm going to Fowler Town to visit my Aunt Mildred," Anna replied, returning the deputy's smile.

"You didn't mention it last night," Ward said.

"I saw no reason to."

"I'd rather you not go. At least, not on this particular trip."

"These two gentlemen have already told me of the money shipment, and I assume they're guarding it," Anna said.

"Yes, these are the two men I was telling you about, last night," Ward said. "These are the Crockett brothers. Will, Gid, this pretty young lady is Anna Burke."

"Well, Mr. Will and Mr. Gid Crockett, from what Ward has told me, I couldn't ask for better protection," Anna said.

"I can't talk you into waiting until tomorrow?" Haller asked.

"I really need to take this one," Anna said. She smiled again at the deputy. "And if these two gentlemen are as . . . efficient as you indicated they were last night, I'm sure I will be safe. Are you going to miss me, Ward?"

"I'll be counting the minutes," Ward replied, surrendering to the fact that he wouldn't be able to make her change her mind.

"Folks," the driver called down to his passengers, "if you'll climb aboard now, we'll get this trip underway."

Ward hurried over to open the door to the coach, then helped Anna board. Will and Gid smiled at the special attention the pretty young woman was getting from the deputy, then they climbed in behind her.

Chapter Eleven

"Heah!" the driver shouted, his shout followed by the pistol-like report of the cracking whip.

As the coach got underway, Anna waved one last time at Deputy Haller.

A young boy began running alongside the coach, keeping up with it as long as it was still in town.

"Bye, Daddy, bye!" the boy shouted, waving at the driver.

"Bye, Timmy," the driver called back down to him. "You take good care of your mama while I'm gone now."

"I will!" Timmy called back, stopping now and leaning over to put his hands on his knees, breathing hard from the effort of trying to keep up with the coach.

"That was Timmy, the driver's little boy," Anna said.

"You know him, you spoke to the man from the bank," Will said. "Do you know everyone in town?"

Anna chuckled. "Well, what with papa being a doctor, and me helping him, I suppose I do know a lot of people."

"I saw the way you and the deputy exchanged waves," Will said. "I'd say that young man likes you."

"He's very nice," Anna said without further comment on the subject. "So, you two are brothers, are you?"

"Well, that's what mom told me," Will said. "But I've always sort of figured she found Gid under a toadstool somewhere."

"Whoowee, it must have been a large toadstool," Anna said, with a little laugh.

While the conversation was going on between Will, Gid, and Anna, another discussion was taking place upon the driver's seat.

"Looks like we'll have good weather for the trip," Sonny Taylor said. Sonny was a former soldier, who for the last year, had been working as the shotgun guard.

"That's good," Tony Stallings, the driver, replied. "There's nothin' worse 'n sittin' up here, holding slick ribbons to these critters in the middle of a rain storm."

Sonny chuckled. "It ain't no better ridin' on this side."

"I tell you the truth, Sonny, I kind 'a wish the doctor's daughter wasn't travelin' with us this mornin'," Tony said. "Someone should have told her we're carryin' a money shipment."

"Hell, Tony, someone did tell her. I seen them two passengers talkin' to her, 'n the deputy too. Besides which, it was in the paper. She's just bound 'n determined to make this trip is all."

"Well, she bought a ticket, so we ain't got no right to say she can't ride with us," Tony said.

"That may be, but it kind'a makes you wonder why they put that story in the paper 'bout us carryin' all this money, don't you think?"

"If you just think about it, you'll know why. The two men we're a' carryin' this morning are the Crockett brothers. I reckon you've heard of them."

"Well yeah, hell yes I've heard of 'em, they're like super bounty hunters or something and . . . wait a minute. I'll be damn. We're bait."

"Feel somewhat like the worm on a hook, do you?" Tony asked with a little chuckle.

* * *

A little over two hundred miles west of Tilden, Martin Baker, because he had been present in the saloon the last time Cedric Warren was seen alive, was asked to participate in the inquest.

Baker, who the sheriff and others thought was a man named Morris, sat in the sheriff's office with the other witnesses, as the sheriff asked his questions. He questioned, first, those who had been in the poker game with Cedric.

"Mr. Guthrie, how much money did you lose in the poker game?" Sheriff Collins asked.

"About thirty dollars," Guthrie replied.

Further investigation determined that Kern lost forty dollars, while Underhill lost over a hundred dollars.

"How did you feel about losing so much money?" the sheriff asked.

"How do you expect me to feel?" Underhill replied. "That was all the money I had saved for the last six months."

"Do you think Cedric Warren was cheating?" the sheriff asked.

"Well, if he was, he was awful damn good at it, because there didn't nobody never catch 'im doin' it."

Baker was the last one to be interviewed.

"You aren't under any suspicion, Mr. Morris," the sheriff said. "The hotel clerk watched you go to bed last night, and he woke you up this morning. But you were in the saloon when the other four were playing poker, were you not?"

"Yes, I was having my supper."

"And you could overhear the conversation?"

"Bits and pieces of it," Baker said. "I didn't hear enough

of it to talk about."

"Did you, and this is very important, Mr. Morris, but did you hear anyone say anything to Mr. Warren, that would make you think any of them could be angry enough to kill him?"

The other three poker players, Guthrie, Kern, and Underhill looked anxiously toward Baker.

Baker shook his head. "No, I can't say as I did. There was nothin' more goin' on than any other poker game I've ever played in, or just watched."

The three poker players looked at Baker with a sense of relief.

The findings of the inquest suggested that Cedric Warren, a cowboy employed by the Rocking R Ranch, was killed on the road on his way back to the bunkhouse, by person, or persons unknown.

"Will you be stayin' in Frio, Mr. Morris?" Underhill asked, as the participants in the hearing left the sheriff's office.

"No, I'm heading for Pettus. I have a friend there, who has offered me a job," Baker said.

"How 'bout havin' dinner with the three of us before you go?"

"Oh, I don't know," Baker said. "I had supper last night and breakfast this mornin'. I don't know as I've got enough money to have another meal in a restaurant.

I've got me some bacon I'll prob'ly cook out on the trail."

Underhill smiled. "Me 'n Kenny 'n Bert will buy your dinner for you. We want to thank you for bein' honest. I think Sheriff Collins was tryin' to pin that murder on one of us. But hell, Cedric was a good friend to all of us, 'n it's bad enough he got killt, let alone that the sheriff might a' thought one of us done it."

"Well, I have to admit that bein' near broke, the idea of gettin' another meal I didn't have to cook over a camp fire is pretty appealin'. I thank you for your offer."

Back in Tilden, within a few minutes after the coach left town, it had achieved a gentle rocking on the through braces. The sound of the hoofbeats, and even the squeaking of the coach and the rolling buzz of the wheels, soothed their passage.

Anna took out a book and began to read.

"What are you reading?" Will asked.

"*Anna Karenina,* it's a book by Tolstoy."

"Is it a good book?"

"Oh, yes, I think it is a wonderful book," Anna said. "Ward gave it to me for my birthday."

"Deputy Haller seems quite taken with you, Miss Burke," Will said.

Anna smiled. "He's a very nice man, perhaps the nicest I've ever met. I just wish he . . ." Anna stopped in mid-sentence.

"There's a problem with him?"

"Yes. Well, not a problem, exactly. It's just that I feel he is somewhat intimidated by Papa. I get the idea that he feels like Papa won't think he's good enough for me. Papa thinks the world of him, I know that, because he's told me so."

"Give the deputy some time, I've got a feeling he'll figure it out," Gid said.

"I certainly hope so."

"I know that Deputy Haller was concerned about you coming with us today, and properly so."

"Do you think it's likely, that someone might actually attack us?" Anna asked.

"Oh, yes, ma'am, I think it is considerably more than just likely," Will replied.

"Oh, dear, I may have been a bit intemperate in my insistence to take the coach this morning."

"If we are attacked, get down onto the floor," Will said. "Stay as low as you can."

"I . . . yes, I will. Thank you."

Chapter Twelve

About five miles ahead of the coach, Jess Felton, Paddy O'Neal, Ed Kildeer, and Julius Paxton were waiting behind a rock outcropping that lay alongside the Tilden to Fowler Town road.

"Ha! Look at that!" Paxton said. "I just pissed a grasshopper offen o' that briar bush."

"Damn, Paxton, ain't you got no better sense than to take a piss where folks is eatin'?" O'Neal asked.

"There ain't hardly nobody still a' eatin' 'ceptin' you," Paxton said.

"Knock it off, both of you," Felton said. "We ain't got time to be a'doin' no fightin'."

"How much longer do you think it'll be before the coach gets here?" O'Neal asked.

"I figure it'll be here in the next half-hour or so," Felton said. "Now remember, O'Neal and Kildeer, I want you two to go on back down the road a piece, 'n when the stagecoach passes you by, come out behind it."

"What are we s'posed to do then?"

"Just start followin' it."

"What if they see us trailin' along behind 'em like that?"

"It won't make no never mind, they'll just think you're travelers on the road. Just kind of poke along behind it so as they don't get suspicious, 'n then follow it 'till it gets here. When it gets here, me 'n Paxton will ride out in front of it, 'n that way we'll have 'em boxed in."

"What if they don't stop?" Kildeer asked.

"Oh, they'll stop all right," Felton said with an evil grin. "We'll shoot the driver and the shotgun guard, 'n that'll stop 'em."

"What if there's someone inside the coach?" O'Neal asked.

"There ain't likely to be nobody other'n a couple of drummers 'n maybe a woman."

"I hope it's a good-lookin' woman," O'Neal said.

"It don't make no difference iffen she's a fine lookin' woman or not. We ain't goin' to be stickin' around to enjoy the view. Soon as we get the money, we'll be gettin' outta here."

"I'll be goin' down to Mexico," Kildeer said.

"Why the hell would you want to go some'ers where you can't even speak the language?" O'Neal asked.

"On account of with the money we'll be gettin' from this job, I could near 'bout live like a king for the rest 'o my life. 'N it won't matter none whether I can speak Mexican or not, 'cause damn near ever' one of them Mexicans can speak 'Merican."

"I'm gettin' too old for this," Tony Stallings said. "My back gets to hurtin' with me sittin' up here like this." He repositioned himself on the driver's seat to take some of the pressure off his back. He snapped the reins of the six-horse team, just to remind them that he was still in charge. "You asked Sally to marry you, yet?"

"No, I ain't asked her yet."

"When are you plannin' on doin' that?"

"What are you, her pa, wantin' to know my intentions?"

Tony chuckled. "Hell, Sonny, I know your intentions. But my question is, when are you goin' to be askin' her to marry you?"

"Matter of fact, I'm plannin' on askin' her this weekend. She's invited me to go to church with her 'n her family, 'n I'm goin' to ask her right after church is over."

"Good for you. I'll tell Jennie. She'll be wantin' to come up with some kind of a get-together of all the women to celebrate."

"That would be just real fine of Mrs. Stallings to do that," Sonny said.

Conversation was just as spirited among the passengers.

"I don't know why Ward would feel intimidated," Anna was saying. "He does have two years of college, you know."

"No, we weren't aware of that."

"He's very smart. He was studying to be a lawyer but then his father died, and he had to drop out of school to take care of his mother. She was sickly, even before Mr. Haller died, so there was nothing Ward could do, but come home and look after her."

"Ty seem's awfully taken with your young man," Gid said.

"Ty? You call the sheriff, Ty?"

Will chuckled. "We've been calling him Ty since we were ten years old."

"Oh yes, Ward did say that you and the sheriff were old friends."

Suddenly, the stagecoach came to an unexpected and abrupt stop.

"You folks be alert down there," the driver called out. "Looks like we've got some men here who might cause us a little . . ." That was as far as the driver got before shots rang out.

"They're here!" Will shouted, and he jumped out from one side of the coach, and Gid the other.

"Get down, Miss Burke!" Gid calle[d]

There were two men in front of t[...] and Gid tumbled out of either side o[...] gan shooting. One of the men went [...] turned and galloped away. Then sho[...] them and spinning around Will sa[...] shot one of the two, but the other [...]

"Gid, you keep a lookout," Wil[l...] check on the driver and the guar[d...]

"I've been hit, Will," Gid repli[ed...]

"Gid, no!" Will shouted, and[...] the other side of the coach wh[...] ashen face, leaning against the [...] coach. He was holding his han[d...] about three inches above his k[nee...] through his fingers.

"Go after them, Will," Gi[d...] horses and go after them."

"I'm not leaving you."

"Maybe I can help," Ann[...] from the coach. [...]

"You?"

"Yes, me. It's not like [...]upid." wounds before. I've assi[sted...] his patients," she said. "[...]ed up to check on [...]nd if you in the boot."

don't think you're going to want that."

"All right all right," O'Neal said, as begrudgingly, he began to climb. When he got seated, Will tied him to the seat and then tied his hands.

"Mr. Gid, you get in this coach at once," Anna ordered. "You're starting to bleed through the bandages."

"Do what she says, Gid."

"Oh, yes, a lot of help you've been, having him lift that weight," Anna said, critically. "The strain is more than likely the cause of the bleeding."

"I'm going to round up Kildeer's horse and tie it on to the back of the coach," Will said as he was tending to O'Neal's horse. "No sense in letting the poor thing wander around."

As soon as Will retrieved the horse, he looked into the coach to check on his brother. Gid was sitting in the front seat with his wounded leg stretched out on the seat. Anna was sitting across from him. The wound was covered, but the bandage was red with blood. Anna had applied a tourniquet just above the wound.

"How is he?"

"I think I have the bleeding under control, for now," Anna said. "But we need to get him back to my father as quickly as possible."

"We're on our way," Will said, and climbing up into the driver's seat, he swung the coach around so that they

115

were heading back to Tilden. He lashed the horses into a gallop, and at a full gallop they covered the eight miles back to town in less than half an hour.

When the coach made an unexpected return at a full gallop with two horses tied to the back, it caught everyone's attention.

Their curiosity and concern grew when they saw that it wasn't Tony Stallings driving.

"Tony!" a woman screamed. "Oh, my God, where's my husband?"

The woman began weeping as a nearby woman embraced her. The coach swept by, then stopped in front of the doctor's office. Dr. Burke drawn by the commotion, had stepped out front.

"Oh! Anna!" the doctor shouted. "Is my daughter . . ."

"I'm here, Papa," Anna called out from the coach. "And I'm fine, but I have a badly wounded man with me."

By now, several citizens of the town had gathered around the doctor's office to see what was going on.

"Why are you driving? What happened to Tony and Sonny?" someone called, as Will brought the coach to a halt, then set the brake and wrapped the reins around the brake handle.

"You don't have to ask," another answered. "I suspect that's them lyin' on top of the coach."

"Anna!" a worried Deputy Haller called out, just now

rushing to the coach. "Are you all right?"

"I'm fine," Anna replied, standing by as Ward helped Will get Gid from the coach.

"My God, what happened here?" Sheriff McMurtry asked as he hurried to the scene.

"We were hit," Will said. "We saw four men but two got away. That's Kildeer on top with the driver and the guard, and the man tied to the seat is Paddy O'Neal."

"What about Gid?" Ty asked.

"It's his leg. It would have been a lot worse if Anna hadn't been with us."

Gid put his arm around Will's shoulder and they took one step before Gid called out. "I don't think this is going to work."

"I'll help," the deputy said, and he took Gid's other arm and put it around his shoulder. Then, with two men supporting him, they were able to get Gid into the doctor's office.

Chapter Thirteen

"Get him up on the table," Dr. Burke directed, once Will and Ward got Gid into the operating room of the doctor's office.

When Gid was on the table, Ward stepped back.

"I'd better go see if Ty needs me," he said.

Dr. Burke began to remove the bandages from Gid's leg.

"Anna, honey, you did a good job stopping the bleeding. Did you loosen the tourniquet, from time to time?"

"It only took half an hour to get back, so I loosened it once, then counted to sixty before I tightened it again," Anna said.

Dr. Burke nodded. "Good job. You probably saved his life, now let's see if I can save his leg." Dr. Burke looked up to see that Will was still standing there. "And who are you?"

"His name is Will, Papa. This is Gid Crockett, and

Will is his brother."

"Ah yes, the Crockett Brothers, the two men Ward was telling us about. All right, Will, help me lift this man up just enough so that Anna can pull his pants off. But first, we'd better take off his boots."

"Wait a minute, Doc," Gid said when he heard the comment. "You're goin' to pull my pants off in front of the lady?"

"Young man, it's either pull off your pants or take off your leg. Now which shall it be."

"I won't look until your modesty is preserved," Anna said with a smile.

"All right, Doc, then pull 'em off," Gid said.

After that was done, Dr. Burke was able to get a closer look at the wound which, even now, was bleeding. Dipping a cloth into some alcohol, he paused for just a minute, then looked at Gid.

"I'm going to have to clean the wound. It's probably going to sting a little."

Gid laughed.

"What's funny?" Dr. Burke asked.

"Doc, I'm lying here with a bullet hole in my leg, it's hurting like hell, and you tell me something is going to sting a little?"

"Good attitude," Dr. Burke said with a little chuckle, as, using alcohol, he began washing away the blood so he could get a closer look at the wound.

"Damn! That stings more than a little," Gid said. "Sorry 'bout my language, Miss Burke."

"Think nothing of it," Anna said with a smile. Then to her father, "The bullet is still in there, Papa; it didn't go all the way through."

"Then we'll have to dig it out."

"Now, *that* sound like a little more than a sting," Gid said.

"We can take care of that," Dr. Burke said, with a nod toward Anna.

Anna took down a bottle of chloroform then, dropping a few drops onto a gauze mask, she held it so that Gid could breathe in the vapors. Dr. Burke waited, with probe and forceps until Gid was quiet.

"He's out," Anna said.

Dr. Burke used the probe until he found the bullet, then, laying the bloody probe aside, he stuck the long, very narrow, extractor into the bullet hole.

"I've got it," he said. "I think I can pull it through the entry path without any more tissue damage."

Will was watching intently as Anna added a few more drops of chloroform, and Dr. Burke worked slowly, and precisely until he removed the forceps from the wound with the bullet in its grasp.

"Here it is," he said triumphantly, before dropping the

bullet into a pan of water. A little trickle of blood worked its way up through the water from the bullet.

"Now, my dear, you can stop with the anesthesia."

Dr. Burke thoroughly cleaned the wound with alcohol, then, with Anna's help, applied a bandage.

"So, what do you think, Doc?" Will asked, when the procedure was finished. "There's no danger of him losing his leg, is there?"

"Not unless sepsis sets in. But I'll be monitoring his heart rate, and temperature. If that remains normal, then all he will have to do is let it heal."

"Thanks, Dr. Burke. I can't tell you how much I appreciate that."

"Actually, you should thank Anna. She kept your brother from bleeding to death."

"Miss Burke, you have my undying appreciation, and frankly, my admiration that you knew what to do."

"Hey!" Gid called out, regaining consciousness at that moment. "Where's my pants?" He started thrashing around, as Dr. Burke tried to restrain him.

"Just hold on here, Mr. Crockett," the doctor said. "If you lie still, you'll feel a lot better."

"What happened?"

"Dr. Burke just pulled a bullet out of your leg," Will said.

"Oh, right, I remember now. Would it be all right if I

just sort of took a nap here for a few minutes?"

"We don't mind at all," Dr. Burke said. "In fact, that's the best thing you could do." Then he spoke to Will. "He'll be groggy for a couple of hours. When he feels up to it, we'll move him from the operating table to one of my beds."

Ty McMurtry stood out in front of a white, two-story house. There was a large tree in the front yard and hanging from a perfectly horizontal limb of the tree was a rope swing. The grass had been worn away under the swing, indicative of its use by the Stallings children.

This was Tony Stallings house, and though he knew that Jenny Stallings was aware of her husband's fate, he felt obligated to visit with her. It wasn't a visit he was looking forward to, especially as he felt responsible. He had set a trap to catch the Felton gang; he had not taken into consideration the possibility that the trap could backfire and cause both the driver and the shotgun guard to be killed.

When Ty knocked on the door, it was answered by Ethyl Joyce, Stallings' next-door neighbor.

"Hello, Sheriff, you've come to visit with Jennie," Mrs. Joyce said.

"Yes."

"I'm sure she will appreciate it. Sally McCord is

here too. You might know that she was about to marry Sonny Taylor."

When Ty went into the living room, he saw the two women sitting together on the sofa. They were holding hands, and they were both weeping, their sobbing visible, but not audible. Tony Stallings' three children, two girls and a boy were sitting on the floor in front of the sofa. All three showed evidence of having been crying, though now they were just sitting there with incredibly sad expressions on their faces.

"Mrs. Stallings, Miss McCord, I can't begin to tell you how sorry I am." Ty took a hand from each of them.

"Thank you, Ty, it was sweet of you to come," Jennie said.

Jennie's gracious response caused Ty to feel an even greater sense of responsibility over what had happened.

"If there is anything, I can do for either one of you ladies, please let me know."

"Is it true that you captured one of the killers?" Sally asked.

"Yes, we did."

"Then here is what you can do for us," Sally said. "You can make sure that that miserable excuse for a man pays for what he did."

"I will promise you that," Ty said.

"My daddy's never coming home again," the boy said.

"Yes, Timmy, I'm afraid you are right."

"Mama says he's in heaven," the youngest daughter said.

"He is indeed, darlin', he is indeed," Ty replied.

As Ty was visiting with Jenny, Sally, and the three children, Deputy Haller stepped into Dr. Burke's office. He was leading an angry looking Paddy O'Neal.

"Hello, Ward," Anna said.

"Hi, Anna," Haller replied with a broad smile. Then he turned his attention to Dr. Burke.

"Doc, this is Paddy O'Neal," the deputy said. "He was part of the gang that killed Tony and Sonny, and now he says he needs some medical attention, seeing as how he was shot. But I looked at his arm, and to me it doesn't seem like anything more than a scratch."

"I can guarantee it's more than a scratch," O'Neal said. "It hurts like hell."

"Let me take a look," Dr. Burke said.

He had O'Neal take off his shirt, revealing a shallow crease in his left arm, about half-way between his elbow and his shoulder.

"It's just a surface wound, but we'll need to keep it from getting infected."

Returning to the alcohol, he began cleaning the wound.

O'Neal winced. "Damn, Doc, what are you doing?

That hurts!"

"Take it like a man, O'Neal," Wade said.

After cleaning the wound, Dr. Burke applied a bandage.

"That's it? That's all you're going to do?" O'Neal complained.

"I suppose I could amputate your arm," Dr. Burke said.

"Amputate? Wait a minute, does that mean cut off my arm?"

"I'm pretty good at it. I had to do it several times, during the war."

"I don't want to lose my arm but seems to me like you ought to do more than just rub somethin' on it."

Wade chuckled. "That's all he needs to do, O'Neal. We only have to keep you alive long enough to hang you."

"What? You got no right to talk to me like that," O'Neal replied in a grouchy voice.

"Come on, you're going back to the jail," Wade said. "Anna, Doc," he added with a nod of his head.

"Will, the sheriff asked me to bring you with me when I go back. He wants to ask you a few questions."

"I expect he does," Will said.

Will walked back down to the sheriff's office with Wade and the prisoner.

"I thought you took O'Neal down to get treated by the doctor," Sheriff McMurtry said when they walked into the jail.

"I did," Wade replied, puzzled by the sheriff's comment.

"And yet he's back, and he still has both arms. I was hoping there'd be an amputation."

"What?" O'Neal said. "Why the hell is ever' one talkin' about, takin' off my arm?"

"It doesn't matter anyway, O'Neal. You can hang with one arm as well as two."

O'Neal gulped. "You can't hang me. Not without no trial, you can't. It's a'gin' the law."

"Yes, and you are such a stickler for the law," Ty said. "I just left Jennie Stallings, or should I say the widow Stallings, seeing as you killed her husband. Sally McCord was there too. She was planning on marrying Sonny Taylor, only she can't now on account of you killed him too."

"They was four of us. It was some of them others that done the killin', not me."

"Put 'im back in his cell, Ward," Sheriff McMurtry ordered, disgustedly. "I can't stand to even look at the son of a bitch."

Ty turned to Will. "How's Gid?"

"He's doing well, thanks to Anna Burke and what she did for him right after he got shot," Will said. "The doc says that if sepsis doesn't set in, he should do just fine."

Chapter Fourteen

Of the four men who attack the stage coach, only two, Jess Felton and Julius Paxton escaped, unscathed. They retreated to their hide-out cabin. Felton was very familiar with the cabin, because it had once belonged to his mother, and he had lived here until his mother died. Then, after she died, he had gone to live with his uncle. Technically the cabin belonged to him anyway, as his mother was now dead, and his father was serving a life sentence in the state penitentiary in Huntsville.

"Damn, we never had a chance. It was like they was waitin' on us," Paxton complained.

"They was waitin' on us," Felton said. "Didn't you recognize them two?"

"You mean the ones that was shootin' at us? No, I ain't never seen either one of 'em before," Paxton replied. "You mean you've seen 'em?"

"No, I ain't never seen 'em, but I've heard 'em described. They's brothers, 'n one of 'em is regular size 'n one of 'em is a real big son of a bitch. I'd be willing to bet money that they was the Crockett brothers, Will 'n Gid."

"Yeah? Well which one of 'em is the big 'un?" Paxton asked with a little chuckle. "On account of, I shot him, 'n he won't be no trouble no more."

"That's good," Felton said. "But they killt Kildeer and O'Neal."

"No, I seen O'Neal. He warn't no more 'n shot in the arm."

Felton took a bottle of whisky from a cabinet and poured a drink for himself and Paxton.

"The problem is, word's for sure goin' to get out now that we was the ones that done this. That means we're goin' to have to be careful when we start goin' into the towns here 'n there, lookin' for a couple of new men."

"And the worst thing is, we got one of our fella's killt 'n one hurt, 'n we didn't get one red cent of that money," Paxton said.

"There warn't no money," Felton said.

"What do you mean, there warn't no money? You seen it yourself, the paper said they was fifteen thousand dollars bein' took on the stagecoach."

"Yeah, I know that's what the paper said, but I believe it was a set up," Felton said. "I'm thinkin' now that they was just sayin' there'd be money so's we would go after it. I don't think there was money. They was just settin' a trap."

"Yeah, you might be right," Paxton said. "'Cause they sure come tumblin' out of that coach fast. The funny thing is, they got the driver and the shotgun guard killt. 'N the way I look at it, it's as much their fault them two men was killt, as it is our'n."

"I say we lay low here for a few days, then we'll go get us two or three more men, 'n get back into business," Felton said.

"Yeah, but get back into business doing what?"

"Finding some place to get money," Felton said. "But, even before we do that, we have some other business to take care of first."

"What other business?" Paxton asked.

"You might say that it's the business of settlin' accounts with the Crocketts."

"I told you, I done killt one of 'em," Paxton said.

"Then we'll take on the other'n."

Gid was still in the doctor's office, but he was out of bed now, with his left leg stretched out on the chair in front of him.

"They're holding the funeral today?" Gid asked.

"Yes, they're holding both of them at the same time," Anna said.

129

"I want to go," Gid said.

"Young man, I'm not sure that's too good of an idea," Dr. Burke said. "You're still pretty weak and susceptible to infection."

"Doc, I can't help but feel somewhat responsible for those two men getting killed. It was partly my job to protect them, and I didn't. I don't care if I wind up losing my leg, I'm going to their funeral."

"Papa, we can fit Mr. Crockett with a crutch, and I'll look out for him."

Dr. Burke smiled. "Well, if he must go, we can do better than a crutch."

"The wheelchair," Anna said with a broad grin.

"Yes." Dr. Burke went into the back of his office building, then reappeared a moment later, pushing a wheelchair.

"Here you go, young man," Dr. Burke said to Gid. "You can propel yourself, or if you're lazy, you can get someone to push you." He nodded toward Will.

"It'll be like pushing a loaded wagon, but I'll do what I can," Will said with a smile.

Practically the entire town turned out for the joint funeral of Tony Stallings and Sonny Taylor. The driver's widow, Jennie and their three children, Molly, Timothy and Dolly, sat in the front row of the church. Jennie wiped at her eyes and kept one arm around Molly and the other around Dolly. Timothy, who was the oldest of the three children tried hard not to cry.

There were two coffins on catafalques in front of the church, one for Tony Stallings and the other for Sonny Taylor. The shotgun guard had no family in town, so Sally McCord took the roll of grieving family. Like Jennie and her children, Sally occupied the front row of the church.

The pastor, Reverend E.D. Owen, began to speak. "The two men we have come to bury today were two of the finest gentlemen it has ever been my pleasure to meet. We offer our love and our condolences to Tony's wonderful family, his wife, Jennie, and his children, Molly, Timothy, and Dolly. Some may say that Sonny had no family, but they would be wrong. Sonny Taylor was loved by all, and thus we could rightfully say that all of Tilden is his family, and we especially offer our condolences to Miss Sally McCord, who but for cruel fate, would have become Mrs. Sonny Taylor.

"And now we pray, 'Lord our God, the Ruler of life and death, have mercy on us and lead us to faith in our Lord Jesus Christ, our Saviour so that, having completed our journey we may become partakers of the resurrection of the righteous, for the sake of our Lord Jesus Christ.'

"As it has begun to rain, we will continue our visitation here, in the church, until the rain stops and we can inter the last, mortal remains of our departed brothers."

"It isn't raining, Reverend Owen," Timothy said aloud. "That's just God's tears. He's crying."

"God is weeping. Yes, young man, indeed that is true."

The rain lasted but a short time, then everyone went outside to the church burial ground.

After the interment, the mourners gathered in the ball room of the Morning Star hotel for the reception and dinner, provided by the citizens of Tilden in honor of the two men.

Although most of the funeral goers were moving around, offering condolences to the widow and Sally McCord, Gid's wheelchair was sitting on one side of the room. Will had taken a chair from one of the tables and was sitting beside his brother.

"It's too bad we never got the chance to actually meet these two," Gid said. "The way the town has turned out for them, they must have been a couple of very good men."

"Ty and Ward certainly speak well of them," Will said.

"When there is room without crowding anyone, push me over there so I can offer my condolences," Gid said.

Will and Gid sat there for a short while longer, then Will saw the opportunity for them to approach the grieving parties.

"Mrs. Stallings, Miss McCord, my brother and I want to tell you how sorry we are about what happened," Will said.

"You two were on the coach with my husband, weren't you?" Jenny asked. She looked at Gid. "And you got shot."

"Yes, ma'am," Gid replied.

"I'm told that you killed one of the murderers, and that another is in jail."

"Yes, ma'am."

"Why didn't you kill the bad men before they killed Daddy?" Timothy asked.

"Believe me, young man, I certainly wish we had," Will replied.

After exchanging a few more words with Jennie, Sally, and the three children, and also because others were coming to offer their own sympathies, Will and Gid moved out of the way.

"I hate to bother you two with business at a time like this," Ty said, approaching the two brothers then, "but Will, if you could stop by the office, I've got something for you."

"Thanks, Ty, I'll come down to your office as soon as this gathering breaks up," Will said.

After delivering Gid back to Dr. Burke's office, where a quick examination showed that Gid was none the worse for his outing, Will went to the sheriff's office. Ward was sitting behind the desk reading *The Brothers Karamazov* by Fyodor Dostoyevsky.

"Good book?" Will asked.

"It's a little dark," Ward said, laying the book face down on his desk. "Ty's in the back, talking to O'Neal."

"All right if I go back there?" Will asked.

"Sure, I don't think he would mind."

As Will stepped back into the part of the building that held the jail cells, he could hear Ty talking.

"I'm going to ask you again," Ty said. "Where is Felton? Where is he hiding out?"

"I don't have to tell you nothin'," O'Neal was saying.

"It might go easier on you, if you would cooperate."

"You can ask until you're blue in the face, I ain't tellin' you nothin'."

Will chuckled. "Sounds like a really interesting conversation."

"I'm wasting my time with him," Ty said with a dismissive wave of his hand. "Doesn't matter, he's going to hang anyway."

"I wouldn't be so sure if I was you," O'Neal said. "Felton has said before that if one of us was to get caught, the rest of us would come rescue him."

"The 'rest of you' is only two men now," Ty said.

"I ain't worried none," O'Neal said.

"Come on out front, Will, I've got a voucher for bringing this one in, and killing Kildeer," Ty invited.

"That's appreciated," Will said.

"I almost feel sorry for the son of a bitch," Ty continued, "counting on Felton to do something for him."

"I guess everyone has to hang onto something."

"I suppose so. I wish it would have been Felton that you killed."

"I have a pretty good feeling we'll get another chance at him," Will said.

"I think you may be right. In the meantime, here's your voucher. Money well spent by the state of Texas, if you ask me."

Will took the state voucher to the Bank of Tilden and submitted it to the teller for the two hundred and fifty dollar reward for each of the two men, O'Neal and Kildeer.

"That's a lot of money to be carrying around, Mr. Crockett. Are you sure you wouldn't want to open an account here?"

"I think that would be a pretty good idea, but half of this money belongs to my brother, so, maybe I should talk to him first."

Half an hour later, Will returned to the bank.

"My brother agrees," he said. "We want to open a joint account."

"Very good, sir," the teller said with a practiced smile. "Five hundred dollars in the joint account of . . ."

"No, that would be two thousand four hundred dollars," Will said.

The teller looked up in surprise. "But, sir, your reward was for only five hundred dollars."

"This reward was, but we intend to add some money to it," Will replied as, with a smile, he laid the cash money before the shocked teller.

"Yes, sir!" the teller replied, now with a broad smile. "We can open an account for you right away."

Will returned to the doctor's office to report to Gid on the bank transaction. "I held back fifty dollars for each of us," Will said as he handed him his share.

"I want you to help with something," Gid said. "I want you to convince the doc that I could be fitted up with a crutch."

"Why do you want a crutch?"

"Because if I had a crutch, you could help me go down to The Tinderbox. I'm dying for a beer."

Leaving Gid in the room where he had been staying, Will went into the doctor's office where he saw Dr. Burke and Anna sterilizing some of his instruments.

"How about it, Doc? Would it be all right if my brother and I go down and have a beer?"

"I don't have a problem with that," Dr. Burke said. "Anna, get the wheelchair."

"He'd rather have a crutch, if that's all right," Will said.

"I suppose that would be all right, as long as he doesn't put too much strain on his leg," Dr. Burke replied. "I think it would be good for Gid to get away from here, for a while. His patience with confinement is running a little thin."

Chapter Fifteen

"Oh, you're up and walking around!" Fancy said happily, as she greeted Gid when he came hobbling into the saloon. "We all heard how you got shot during the stagecoach holdup, and how Miss Burke probably saved your life. I was so worried about you."

"If it didn't hurt so much, I'd say it was almost worth getting shot to have a pretty girl worrying about me," Gid replied with a broad smile.

"Here, put your other arm on my shoulder and let me help you up to the bar. Or would you rather sit at a table?" Fancy said.

"The bar's fine. I've been sittin' and lyin' down so much these last few days, that it feels good to be on my feet. But I'd sure welcome puttin' my arm around you," Gid said, his smile broadening.

"Oh, so I'm not good enough for you anymore?" Will

teased.

"You'll do in a pinch," Gid said. "But I'll take help from a pretty girl, anytime I can get it."

Fancy walked alongside Gid as they approached the bar.

"Damn, Gid, you sure are getting a lot of attention," Will said. "I'm beginning to get a little jealous."

Gid laughed. "Well, heck, all you have to do is get yourself shot. It worked for me."

Gid, Will, and Fancy reached the bar, where Gid made the order.

"Clyde, my big brother and I will have a beer, and give the little lady whatever she wants to drink."

"Fancy's drink you'll have to pay for, but you two get a free drink for taking care of two of the Felton gang."

"Thanks," Will said. "Too bad we didn't get Felton himself."

"You'll get him," Clyde said. "I have confidence that you will."

Doodle, Harry and Jaco, the three men who had tangled with Gid before, were sitting at their usual table when Will and Gid came into the saloon.

"There's that big son of a bitch that we had trouble with the other day," Doodle said.

"He ain't gettin' around all that well now, is he?" Jaco asked.

"I'd say he ain't," Doodle replied. "I think I'll go have a few words with him."

Doodle got up and approached the bar where Gid was talking to Fancy.

"Hey, big man, how does it feel to be a cripple?" Doodle taunted.

"It doesn't feel all that good," Gid replied.

Doodle gave a mocking laugh. "Yeah, I just bet it don't."

"Doodle, please go away and leave us in peace. Gid hasn't done anything to you," Fancy said.

"The hell he ain't. He damn near broke my jaw is what he done. Anyhow, me 'n him is just passin' a few words back and forth."

"I'm glad you're concerned about me," Gid said. "But I agree with the young lady here. I'd just as soon you go back to your table and leave us in peace."

Doodle laughed. "Lady? Mister, are you calling this whore a lady? There ain't a man between twenty and sixty in the whole county she ain't slept with."

"It's going to take a little convincing to get you to go away and leave us along, isn't it?" Gid asked.

"Convincin', yeah, that's what it's goin' to take. Only, with you bein' crippled up like you are, I can't see as how you got any convincin' left in you."

Gid lifted his crutch, and in one easy movement, drove the tip of the crutch hard into Doodle's solar plexus. With a swooshing sound, Doodle grabbed his stomach and bent forward, then fell to the floor gasping for breath.

"I expect you two had better see to your friend," Will said.

"Harry, Jaco, you scoop up Doodle, 'n the three of you stay out of trouble, or you'll wind up spendin' the night in jail again," Clyde said.

"Yeah," one of the other patrons said. "If you do that, you'll be keepin' company with that son of a bitch that killt Tony 'n Sonny."

"You're talkin' about Paddy O'Neal, aren't you?" one of the other saloon customers asked.

"Paddy O'Neal, yeah."

"He's got no business bein' in jail."

"Coy, what do you mean, he's got no business bein' in jail? The son of a bitch killt Tony Stallings and Sonny Taylor, two of the finest men you'd ever want to know," one of the other saloon patrons said.

"Yeah, Amon, that's what I'm talkin' about. Instead of lyin' on his ass in jail, eating food that the city has to pay for, he should be hanging from the hoist bar down at the livery stable."

"Nah, when the court finds the son of a bitch guilty, they'll build a nice gallows for him, and ever' one in town can come watch him swing. And I'm goin' to be standin' in the front row," Amon said.

A few minutes later Doodle, Harry, Jaco, Amon, and Coy left the saloon, still talking about what a great day it was going to be when the whole town could turn out to watch the hanging of Paddy O'Neal.

"I have to tell you that I agree with them," Will said after they left. "Public hangings aren't my idea of a good time, but Paddy O'Neal needs to hang."

Rebel had been sitting at the same table as Coy and Amon, and when they left, she stepped up to the bar with Fancy, Gid, and Will.

"Clyde, pour this little lady a drink as well," Will said.

"Everyone is saying that you two are heroes," Rebel said.

"Nothing heroic about gettin' shot," Gid said.

"You sure you aren't ready to sit down, Little Brother?" Will asked. "There's a couple of empty tables over there."

"Yeah, I guess it would be better."

The four moved to the empty table.

"Fancy, what's your real name, darlin'," Gid asked. "I know it's not Fancy."

She laughed. "You're right. It's Millie. Millie Jean Sanders."

"What about you?" Will asked Rebel.

"Sara Sue Sanders."

"Sanders?"

"We're sisters," Millie said.

"Sisters? How did you . . ."

"Wind up as whores?" Millie asked.

"I wasn't going to say that."

"No, because you are too nice a man, one of the nicest I've ever met. But it's true, that's what we are."

"It's because of me," Sara Sue said.

"Ma was a drunk, and after pa died, she married again. The man she married was . . ." Millie started, but she was interrupted in mid-sentence by her sister.

"An evil son of a bitch who raped me when I was fourteen years old."

"I caught him in the act and hit him with an andiron. 'Till this day, I don't know if I killed him or not, but we didn't stay around long enough to find out. We ran away from home, I was seventeen and Sara Sue was fourteen. I tried to find me a job that would support us, but finally wound up, going on the line. I hoped to keep Sara Sue from having to do such a thing . . ."

"But I didn't feel right about her feeding us, with no help from me. So, when I turned seventeen years old, I joined her."

Outside a group of people had gathered around Coy Prosser.

"I'm tellin' you right here 'n now, somethin' about that sumbitch down there," he pointed toward the jail, "What he's doin' is, he's a' lyin' in there on his ass enjoyin' hisself. Where's Tony Stallings? Where's Sonny Taylor? I'll tell you where they are. They're lyin' dead, in the cemetery! 'N the reason is because O'Neal killt 'em."

By now the number of townspeople gathered around Coy had grown considerably larger.

"Ever' meal that sumbitch has et since he got 'n jail, we've paid for. Free bed, 'n free food for a murderin' bastard like Paddy O'Neal ain't right."

"No, it ain't!" someone shouted back at him.

"That sumbitch needs to hang!" Coy shouted, again pointing toward the jail.

"Hell, Prosser, don't you think he is goin' to hang?" someone asked.

"Yeah," another said. "They're goin' to try 'im, 'n you know damn well he'll hang."

"I say we don't wait. I say we make certain he hangs, by doin' it ourself!" Coy said.

Doodle had been as condemning of O'Neal as everyone else, but now they were talking lynching. Doodle, whose real name was Simon Gauterot had seen his brother lynched back in Louisiana. As it later developed, his brother was proven to be innocent. He had no doubt about the guilt of Paddy O'Neal, but he didn't want to be part of a lynching.

Both Millie and Sara Sue, for that was how Will and Gid thought of them now, were laughing when Doodle came back into the saloon.

"Where's them two Crockett brothers?" Doodle asked.

"Doodle, don't you be makin' anymore trouble now," Clyde warned.

"I ain't makin' no trouble," Doodle said. "I'm here to . . ." he saw Will and Gid sitting at the table with Fancy and Rebel, and he hurried over to the table.

"Look here!" he said. "I come to warn you that Coy Prosser is gettin' folks all charged up for a lynchin'. They're plannin' on takin' O'Neal outta jail 'n hangin' 'im."

"Thanks, Doodle," Gid said. "Will, we need to stop this."

"There's no 'we' in this, Gid. You aren't in any condition to get involved, hell you can barely walk by yourself. Millie, I'll give you twenty dollars to walk Gid back to the doctor's place."

"I don't need anything like that," Gid said.

"Why, Gid, are you telling me you wouldn't enjoy taking a walk with a pretty girl?"

Gid smiled. "Well, yeah, I mean if you put it that way." He offered his arm to Millie. "Let's go, girl."

"What are you going to do, Will?" Clyde asked.

"I'm going to go down to the jail and offer my assistance to the sheriff and his deputy, to see if we can stop a lynching."

Chapter Sixteen

Will stepped outside the saloon and watched for a moment as Gid and Millie started back toward Dr. Burke's office, to make certain that they were having no trouble and to see that Gid was actually willing to go back to the doctor's office.

"We don't need no trial. That son of a bitch needs to hang now!"

The disembodied shout came from the middle of a group of men that was gathering in front of Beck's Livery Stable.

Will hurried on down to the sheriff's office.

"Hello, Will, how's Gid doin'?" Sheriff McMurtry asked when Will stepped into the sheriff's office after having run from the saloon. "And what's your hurry?"

"Gid is doing fine, but you aren't," Will replied. "Some hotheads are putting together a lynch mob. They plan on snatching O'Neal out of jail and hanging him."

"Damn!" the sheriff replied.

"Have you any scatter guns?"

"I've got four of 'em."

"Good, that'll give each of us one. Load them with bird shot, not buck. We want to keep them away, not kill them," Will said.

"Give us O'Neal! Give us O'Neal! Give us O'Neal!"

"Hang 'im! Hang 'im high! Hang the son of a bitch."

The chant was coming from a large group of people who were making their way toward the jail. Ward loaded three of the Greener twelve-gauge shotguns with bird-shot, tossing one to Ty and one to Will. Then, so armed, the three men stepped out front to meet the crowd.

"Coy Prosser is leading them," Ty said. "I'm not surprised, he always has been a troublemaker."

There were at least fifteen of them, and they came right up to the front of the sheriff's office then stopped.

"What do you want, Prosser?" Sheriff McMurtry asked.

"You know what we want. We want your prisoner."

"What do you want with him?"

"What do you mean, what do we want with him? We want to hang the sumbitch, that's what we want. Now bring him out here, or we'll come in there 'n get 'im."

"We're not goin' to let you do that," Will said.

"Yeah? How the hell are you plannin' on stoppin' us? They's near twenty of us, 'n they's only three of you. Now you either step aside, or we're a' comin' over you," Prosser shouted, threateningly.

Will pointed the shotgun at Prosser. "I wouldn't do that if I were you."

"Get out of the way! We're comin' through!"

Prosser started forward, and Will pulled the trigger.

"Ahhh!" Prosser screamed, and with his chest red with blood, he went down.

"Oh, my God! He killt Coy!" someone shouted, and the rest of them ran away.

Groaning, Prosser managed to stand up. "My God, you've killt me," he said.

"Come inside, Coy," Ty said. "That's birdshot, not buckshot. We'll start picking shot out of you 'till the doc gets here. Ward, you go get Dr. Burke."

Although Prosser wasn't seriously injured, Dr. Burke explained that all the shot would have to be removed in order to prevent infection from setting in. Fortunately, the charge was light enough that none of the shot penetrated too deeply and they were easy to remove. The only problem was Coy was hit with at least 200 of the 350 pellets in the birdshot shell, so removing them took almost three hours.

As Martin Baker rode into Pettus, he was tired, but he told himself he had a right to be. He had been riding for three weeks, spending most of his nights on the trail and eating most of his meals there too. He had no idea where Felton was, but he knew that Felton had robbed a bank here. Obviously, Felton wouldn't still be here, but this was the last place Baker could put him. And that being the case, Baker decided he would stop his wandering here, and with this as his base, begin his search from this point.

Weathered, rip-sawed lumber buildings faced each other across the main street, consisting of the usual small-town businesses. Some of the businesses appeared to be more substantial than others, the two most substantial being the bank and the Bucket O' Blood saloon. Baker stopped in front of the saloon.

"Hello, cowboy, you're new in town, aren't you? What brings you to the big city of Pettus?" a bar girl asked, greeting him with a practiced smile.

"I'm looking for someone."

"Who you lookin' for, Honey? The reason I asked is I know an awful lot of people here."

"I'm lookin' for Jess Felton."

The girl laughed.

"What are you laughin' at?"

"You, lookin' for Felton. Ever' body's lookin' for 'im,

didn't you know that?"

"I know he robbed a bank here."

"Why then, if you know that, then how come you didn't know ever' one was . . ." the girl paused in mid-sentence. "Wait a minute, you're a bounty hunter, ain't you? That's why you're lookin' for 'im, ain't it? You're after the bounty."

"I might be," Baker agreed. "Do you have any idea where to start lookin'?"

The girl shook her head. "Huh uh, I'm not going to talk about such a thing down here where someone could hear. But, if you'd like to come up to my room, we can talk about it. After."

"After what?"

"After you pay me for visiting my room."

"Yeah, why not? I've been on the trail for damn near a month, spendin' a little time with a willin' woman might be just what I need. What's your name?"

"What do you want it to be, honey?" the girl asked.

"How 'bout callin' yourself Hazel?"

"All right, Hazel it is. Why'd you choose that name?"

"She worked with my mom and was the first one I ever had a poke with."

"Oh, my, did your mom ever find out?"

Baker laughed. "Find out? She's the one that set it up for me."

"What?"

"I told you that Hazel worked with my mom. They were both whores."

Half an hour later as Baker lay in bed, watching Hazel getting dressed, he asked her again about Felton.

"Oh, honey, I don't have no idea where he is," she said.

"What? You said if I came up here, we'd talk about it."

"We are talking about it. You asked me where he was, and I told you I didn't have no idea. That's talkin' about it. 'N you ain't goin' to tell me you didn't have a good time while you was up here."

Baker drew back his hand to hit her but thought better of it.

Hazel gasped and drew back in fear.

Baker forced a laugh. "I ain't goin' to hit you, girl. I was just foolin' with you.

If he hung around town for a while, he might get a lead on how to find Felton, and if he hit her, he was pretty sure nobody would talk to him, even if they did know.

The next evening after the thwarted lynching attempt, Anna invited Ward, Ty, Will, and Gid to join her and her father for dinner.

"I don't know how someone can be so pretty, so smart, and be able to cook," Gid said. "But Ward, you'd better hang on to this one."

"Gid!" Anna said in embarrassment.

"All right, I won't say anything more about it, I'll just eat."

"Doc, how's the man I shot doing?" Will asked. "What's his name?"

"Coy. Coy Prosser. He's going to be just fine, none of the entry wounds appear to be infected. He's home now, having second thoughts about what he almost did."

Ward laughed. "I'm glad he's doing fine, but I doubt that he'll be standing in the front row of any more lynch mobs."

"All he had to do was wait a few days. O'Neal's trial will be coming up soon, and justice will be done," Ty said.

"I hope so," Dr. Burke said. "Jennie is having a very difficult time."

"Well, who can blame her, Papa. She has those three little children to take care of. And don't forget Sally Mc-Cord. She was going to marry Sonny Taylor, and people are overlooking her, because she wasn't married."

"I can't wait to testify at the trial," Gid said.

"Are you going to be able to testify?" Ward asked. "I mean, given your wound."

"The only way you're going to keep me from testifying, is if you put in me jail," Gid said.

Ward chuckled. "As big as you are, Gid, I'd hate to be

the man who tries to keep you from doing whatever it is you want to do, even if you do have a bum leg."

"I'll be testifying too," Anna said.

TRIAL TO COMMENCE ON MONDAY
Much interest is being shown toward the trial that will find the guilt or innocence of Paddy O'Neal, age 24. O'Neal was wounded as he, Jess Felton, and two others attempted to hold up the Tilden to Fowler Town stagecoach. One of the would-be robbers, Ed Kildeer was killed in the attempt. Gid Crockett, who with his brother, Will, prevented the robbery from being successful, was wounded.

Tragically, the driver, Tony Stallings, and the shotgun guard, Sonny Taylor, were killed. Stallings leaves behind his wife, Jennie, their three children, Molly, Timothy, and Dolly.

An attempt to thwart justice by means of a lynching, was foiled by Sheriff McMurtry, Deputy Haller, and Will Crockett.

It is recommended that anyone who wishes to watch the trial arrive early, as it is expected the courtroom will be full.

Martin Baker was enjoying his stay in Pettus. The money he had stolen from the general store, combined with the money he had taken from Cedric Warren enabled him to eat well, drink well, and spend every night with a different woman. He could do all this without leaving the Bucket O' Blood Saloon, and because he was there twenty-four hours a day, he became well known. Also, because he tipped generously, not only the women, but the bartender, he became a favorite customer.

"What I'm wondering is, where did he get all his money?" Sheriff Perkins asked Jake Slater, the bartender. "They say he's spendin' money like a mad man. I mean, where does a cowboy like he says he is, get all the money he's spendin'?"

"Hazel said he's a bounty hunter, so it's more 'n likely some bounty money he collected."

"Hazel?"

Jake laughed. "She was callin' herself Cleo, but you know how she is. She lets the men she's with name her, and Morris named her Hazel."

"What's Morris's first name?" Sheriff Perkins asked.

"I don't know. I've never heard him call himself anything other than Morris."

"That's kind of suspicious in itself, don't you think? I mean, why wouldn't he give his first name?"

"Maybe he figures it would give him an edge over whoever he's lookin' far, if nobody knows his first name."

"I guess it might be. I don't know how, though. I wonder who he's lookin' for."

"Oh, that part's easy. He's lookin' for Jess Felton."

"Yeah? Well, if that's the case, I'm all for him."

Baker was having a drink with Lana, one of the four percentage girls who worked the bar. Lana liked to talk which was good, because he didn't have to offer much to service the conversation. At the moment, Baker's attention was focused on the sheriff who, from the moment he came into the saloon, had been making frequent glances toward him.

Did the sheriff have anything on him?

The sheriff left the bar and came toward Baker. Unobtrusively, Baker dropped his hand to his pistol.

"I hear you're a bounty hunter," the sheriff said.

Baker breathed easier and put both hands on the table. "Yeah, I am, but I don't like to spread it around."

Sheriff Perkins laughed. "I can't say as I blame you. So, you're lookin' for Jess Felton, are you?"

"Yeah. Do you have any idea where I might find him?"

The sheriff shook his head. "I don't have any idea, but seein' as what he did here in Pettus, I think I'll be speakin' for the whole town when I say I hope you find him."

Chapter Seventeen

Felton stood in the open door of the cabin where he had grown up. It made a perfect hideout, it was ten miles from Tilden, and so isolated that nobody would discover it by accident. Behind him Paxton, the only remaining member of his gang, was frying a couple of steaks for their lunch.

For just a moment the smell of the steaks, coming from the same house he had lived in as a boy, reminded him of his mother.

"I just hope and pray that you don't turn out like you father," she would say.

Thinking about it now, Felton couldn't help but smile. His old man wound up in the state penitentiary. Felton had never spent as much as one day behind bars.

"Hey!" Paxton called out to him. "Dinner's ready."

"We've got to get some more people," Felton said as he

came back in to sit at the table. "Do you know anyone we might be able to get to join up with us?"

"Scarborough lives over in Oakville," Paxton replied. "I bet we could get him."

"Ben Scarborough, yeah, I know him, he'd be a good man to get," Felton agreed. "I ain't never been to Oakville, so I could probably get in and outta there without nobody recognizing me. How 'bout you?"

"I've been there, but it's been a long time and I never called no attention to myself."

"All right, come a few more days 'n we'll just pay a visit to Oakville."

The town of Tilden was all abuzz over the upcoming trial for one of the members of the Felton gang. And since he had been involved in the killing of two of the most popular men in town, all were anxious to see justice done. The trial for Paddy O'Neal convened the following Monday. It was set for ten o'clock in the morning, but the doors were due to be opened at eight, and already there was a large crowd gathered in front of the courthouse as so many people wanted to come see the trial. Because nearly everyone in town knew Tony Stallings and Sonny Taylor, many counting one or both of the men as good friends, all were eager to see justice done.

"What's the name of the feller we're tryin'?" another

asked.

"O'Neal. Paddy O'Neal."

"Yeah, that's it, Paddy O'Neal. That's Irish, ain't it?"

"I believe so."

"Yeah, well I hope they hang the Irish son of a bitch. I mean legal, not like them crazy fools tried to do the other day when they took a lynch mob down to the jail."

Sheriff McMurtry arrived then, escorting Jennie Stallings and her three children, as well as Sally McCord.

"Let us through," McMurtry called, and the crowd parted for them, not a few of them offering words of condolences to the two women and the children. McMurtry rapped on the door, and when it was opened, he and his sad little entourage were granted entrance.

Down at the jail, Deputy Ward Haller was looking through the bars of one of the cells.

"You didn't eat your breakfast," Ward said to O'Neal.

O'Neal was sitting on his bunk with the eggs, bacon, and biscuit, uneaten, in front of him.

"I'm not hungry," O'Neal said.

"Well, I can't say as I blame you.

"Hey, deputy, you got 'ny thing I can put in my coffee?"

"Sugar, cream," Ward replied.

"No, somethin' else."

Ward nodded. "Oh, that. Well, ordinarily, we wouldn't

give liquor to prisoners but, you've got quite an ordeal in front of you, so, all right, I'll spice up your coffee a little. But only this once."

"Thanks," O'Neal replied, his voice gruff with fear.

Just across the street from the courthouse, Will, Gid, and Anna were having coffee in The Iron Skillet.

"Look at how many are waiting outside the courthouse. We'll never get in," Anna said.

"You don't have to worry any about that," Will said. "We're witnesses, we won't have any trouble getting in."

True to Will's prediction, they had no trouble getting into the courtroom where they found seats reserved for them.

The gallery was filled with a rather loud buzz of conversation as everyone waited for the trial to begin.

The jury had already been selected and now they filed in, twelve men good and true, to take their seats in the jury box.

"I wish I had been selected for jury duty. I'd make sure O'Neal hangs."

"Jury doesn't sentence, they just find if he is guilty or not."

"Then I would make sure the son of a bitch is found guilty."

Deputy Ward Haller was acting as bailiff, and he

stepped out from a room at the back of the courtroom.

"There's the deputy. What's he doin' up there?"

"All rise!" Ward shouted.

The buzz of conversation stilled, and there was a soft rushing sound of clothing as all stood.

"Here ye, hear ye, hear ye, this court, with Judge Scott Benedict presiding, will now come to order," Ward said, loudly enough for all to hear.

At Haller's pronouncement, Judge Benedict came from his chambers. Judge Benedict's girth was not hidden by his black robe, and his multiple chins added to the effect.

Judge Benedict took his seat behind the judicial bench, then rapped one time with the gavel.

"Be seated."

Again, the rush of clothing, this time accompanied by the squeak of benches bearing the weight.

"This court will now come to order. Mr. Bailiff, would you please tell us why this court has been convened?"

"Your Honor, there comes now before this court, one Paddy O'Neal. Mr. O'Neal is being charged with murder."

"Is the defendant represented by council?" Judge Benedict asked.

The council at the defendant's table stood. "Your Honor, I am David Nolan, authorized by the bar, and appointed by the court to act as defense counsel."

"Who is acting as the prosecutor?" Judge Benedict

asked.

The prosecuting attorney stood. "George Robinson, court appointed prosecuting attorney, Your Honor."

The dialogue between the judge and the lawyers was a formality only. Nolan and Robinson were the only two lawyers in town, and Judge Benedict knew them. Both counselors had acted for the defense and for the state in previous criminal trials, presided over by Judge Benedict.

"With defense counsel and prosecutor present, we may begin this trial. Mr. Prosecutor, please make your case."

Robinson stood, then walked over to directly address the jury.

"Gentlemen of the jury, we are here to seek justice for Tony Stallings and Sonny Taylor," Robinson began. "Tony Stallings leaves behind a grieving wife, and three children, from age nine to thirteen." He paused for a moment. "Two girls and a boy. If you had visited their home during this last week, you would have been struck by the silence. I take that back, it wasn't all silent, because you could hear the sound of weeping.

"Jennie Stallings told me she was trying to be strong for the children, but when the man she loved, the man with whom she had borne three children, and the man who was the breadwinner had been brutally taken from them, it was very hard for her to do. She confessed to me that at night, in her lonely bed, she would cry into the pillow to keep from breaking down before her children.

"Two young girls who, someday, will become brides, but their father will not be there to give them away. And a boy who is now deprived of a personal hero, and a role model to help him become a man.

"All that, gentlemen of the jury, because of the murderous action of this . . . piece of human filth who doesn't deserve to be called a man!" He raised his voice for the last sentence and pointed to Paddy O'Neal.

Several of the women in the gallery could be seen wiping tears from their eyes.

"And, we also seek justice for Sonny Taylor," the prosecutor continued. "Sonny had no family, but there is one citizen, Sally McCord, who, because of a relationship to Sonny, which would have led to marriage, is particularly bereft by the foul murder that took him from her. Sonny was a man of adventure. He had served with Custer, a member of Reno's battalion during the Battle of Little Big Horn, and thus was spared the fate of those brave men who died with Custer. After that, he became a merchant mariner, and when the ship on which he was a crewman sank, he and eight others, survived for eleven days at sea before being rescued.

"Besides being a man of adventure, Sonny was a friend to all. He was generous with his time and money for many civic eleemosynary activities, but that is no more. All that, because of the murderous action of this man!" He pointed to Paddy O'Neal.

Robinson stood for a moment, looking into the faces of all the jury, then he took his seat to the whispered affirmation of those in the gallery.

"Counsel for defense, you may address the court," Judge Benedict said.

"Your Honor, gentlemen of the jury, Paddy O'Neal admits to attempted stagecoach holdup, but denies that he had anything to do with the lamentable murder of the two fine gentlemen Tony Stallings and Sonny Taylor. Indeed, he has expressed his regrets that they were killed in the aborted holdup. But I would remind the jury that there were three other men who attempted to hold up the Fowler Town Stage coach. One of them was killed, and two of them got away.

"In a show of cooperation, Mr. O'Neal, who has no history of murder, has turned state's evidence providing the name of the two men who escaped. One was Julius Paxton, and the other was the notorious Jess Felton, well-known for his reckless disregard for life.

"Given the known presence of these two men, plus the participation of Ed Kildeer, how can we possibly know that the bullets that killed Mr. Stallings, the driver, and Mr. Taylor, the messenger, were energized by Mr. O'Neal, and didn't come from the guns of any, or all, of the other participants? In point of fact, the chances are three to one that the bullets did come from one or more of their guns and didn't come from Mr. O'Neal's gun. In American jurisprudence, you can find a person guilty only if that guilt has been proven not on a three to one possibility, but beyond a shadow of a doubt. With the odds being three to one against my client being the one who killed the driver and the guard, it simply is not possible for you to apply the constitutional standard of beyond a shadow of a doubt to this case and declare Paddy O'Neal guilty of murder. And since in this case the specific charge is murder, and not attempted robbery, you have a constitutional obligation to find Mr. O'Neal, not guilty."

Will, Gid, and Anna testified for the prosecution, and all three told, substantially the same story. The stagecoach came to a sudden and unplanned stop, they heard shooting, then Will and Gid engaged the would-be robbers. When the shooting ended, Gid had been wounded, and they learned that the driver and the shotgun guard were killed by the robbers.

Defense Attorney David Nolan asked all three of the witnesses the same question.

"From whose gun did the bullets come that killed Mr. Stallings and Mr. Taylor?"

All three witnesses gave the same answer.

"I don't know."

There were no defense witnesses, and O'Neal did not testify for himself, so after summation the case was remanded to the jury for deliberation.

Again, Judge Benedict picked up the gavel and rapped it once upon the bench.

"This court is adjourned until after lunch."

Neither Ty nor Ward could be released from their duty at the courthouse, which was guarding the prisoner. Their lunch, and the prisoner's lunch, was provided by The Iron Skillet.

Will, Gid, and Anna returned to the doctor's house for lunch. Before leaving for the courtroom this morning, Anna had put on a beef stew to simmer. Now it was ready to be eaten.

"I wasn't in the courtroom this morning," Dr. Burke said. "How did it go?"

"The jury is deliberating now," Anna said. "It's a cinch they'll find O'Neal guilty."

"What about you, Will? What do you think?"

"I wish I could be as certain as Anna. There's no doubt he'll be found guilty of attempted stage coach robbery, but whether or not he'll be found guilty of murder is another thing."

When they had finished eating, Dr. Burke suggested that Gid let him look at his leg.

"It's doing fine," Gid said.

"I'm sure it is, but I'm going to change the bandage anyway."

"All right," Gid said as he attempted to stand.

"Come with me," Dr. Burke said as he retrieved Gid's crutch.

"Now, don't you all go without me," Gid said, speaking to Will and Anna.

"We won't," Will promised.

Chapter Eighteen

After the enforced silence of the trial, now as they waited for court to reconvene, everyone was now free to talk, and the room buzzed with scores of conversations.

"I don't see how it makes any difference whether his bullets killed both, or even one of the two innocent men, in my mind he's just as guilty. He was a part of a felony in which innocents got killed," Will said.

"And I got shot," Gid added.

"Well maybe if you would have ducked, you wouldn't have gotten shot," Will teased.

"Uh, Will, do I need to point out that I got shot in the leg? If I had ducked, I could have gotten shot in the head."

"Yeah, but as hard as your head is, the bullet would have just bounced off."

"And you two are brothers?" Anna said. "If I had a sister, I would never talk to her the way you two talk to each other."

"It's the only way you can talk to a hard-head like Gid," Will said.

"Besides, if he ever said anything nice to me, his tongue would fall out," Gid replied.

Both brothers laughed, and Anna, seeing that they were just teasing one another, laughed with them.

"There's Deputy Haller," someone said, and looking toward the front of the courtroom they saw the deputy/bailiff coming in.

"All rise," Ward called.

As they had when court was convened that morning, all stood until Judge Benedict took his seat.

"Court is now in session," Benedict said.

Immediately thereafter, the jury filed back in and Judge Benedict turned his attention to them.

"Has the jury elected a foreman?"

The man on the left end of the front row stood. "We have, your honor. I'm Wayne Sinclair and I have the honor of being chosen as the foreman."

"Mr. Sinclair, has the jury reached a verdict?"

"We have, Your Honor."

"Would you please publish the verdict?"

"Your Honor, we find the defendant, Paddy O'Neal, guilty of the charge of first-degree murder."

"All right, you bastard, I'm going to watch you hang!"

The saloon was filled with customers, but the mood was foul.

"It looks like you're doing a lot of business," Gid said.

"Yeah, I am now," Clyde said, putting the two beer mugs before them. "It was empty, and peaceful all the time that the trial was going on. I don't like to turn my back on business, but I almost wish it was that way again. There are a lot of angry folks in here."

"Well as far as I'm concerned, they have every right to be angry," Will said. He shook his head. "I just can't believe the judge didn't sentence that son of a bitch to hang."

Article from *Tilden Free Press*

O'NEAL SENTENCED TO
LIFE IN PRISON

Within the past week, the lives of two of our city's most respected men, Tony Stallings and Sonny Taylor were brutally struck down by soulless brigands in a stage coach robbery attempt. In addition to the murder of Mr. Stallings and Mr. Taylor, Gideon Crockett, a passenger on the coach was wounded.

One of the attackers, Edgar Kildeer, a wanted criminal was killed, and one of the highwaymen, Paddy O'Neal was wounded, and taken prisoner.

O'Neal, in a cowardly attempt to preserve his own life, voluntarily turned state's evidence, naming Jess Felton and Julius Paxton as the two murderers who escaped.

On the very day of the publication of this Extra Edition, a trial was held to determine the fate of O'Neal. A jury of twelve men, good and true, found O'Neal guilty of the murder of Stallings and Turner, and there was universal satisfaction that the widow and three children of the stagecoach driver would see justice served. But alas, that was not to be, for Judge Scott Benedict, in a surprise decision, opted for life imprisonment, rather than death by hanging.

This newspaper interviewed Will and Gideon Crockett, the heroes who thwarted the robbery attempt. Both men expressed their personal dissatisfaction with the judge's decision, stating that "O'Neal should be hanged."

The prisoner will be transferred to the prison at Huntsville on Tuesday next.

In the Bucket O' Blood Saloon in Pettus, Baker was reading the *Bee County Picayune.*

Member of the Felton gang to pay a price for his crimes.

Except for the headline, the story was identical to the one that had run in the *Tilden Free Press.*

The story was both informative, and frustrating. Informative because it validated Baker's belief that Felton was somewhere close by. It was frustrating, because it hadn't given him any more information than he already had, as to how to find Felton.

"Hello, Morris. I see that you've read the story in the *Picayune,*" someone said.

Looking up from the newspaper, Baker saw Sheriff Perkins.

"Yes, I did," Baker said, tapping his fingers against the newspaper.

"He was captured by the Crockett brothers. Have you ever heard of them?"

"Uh, no, I've never heard of them," Baker said.

"Hmm, that's funny, you bein' a bounty hunter, 'n never heard of Will 'n Gid Crockett. Them boys have made quite a name for themselves. Maybe you've heard of the Newcomb and Cassidy gang."

Baker thought of his last sight of Bart Newcomb and

Slim Cassidy, hanging from the gallows in Toyah. And though he had once ridden with

Abner and Slim Newcomb, and their cousins, Bart and Clem Cassidy, he felt a sense of satisfaction, rather than remorse, because they had shot him, and left him for dead, rather than divide their ill-gotten money with him.

"Yeah, I've heard of 'em," Baker said. "I was thinkin' maybe, after I find Felton, I might go look for the Newcombs and the Cassidys."

"Too late for that," Sheriff Perkins said. "Them fellas has done been took care of. The Crocketts killt two of 'em, 'n the other two was hung. But you might go after Martin Baker."

Baker was somewhat shaken to hear the sheriff say his name.

"Who is Martin Baker?" Baker asked.

"Well, turns out he was once a part of the Newcomb and Cassidy gang. They put him in jail, but he killt the jailer 'n escaped. Now there's a five hunnert dollar reward out for 'im, dead or alive."

"Hmm, when I finish with Felton, maybe I'll look for Baker. Do you have a poster with his likeness?"

Sheriff Perkins shook his head. "They don't have no likeness of him."

"Then how am I supposed to find him?"

"That's a good question. I guess the only way Baker

is ever goin' to be caught, is if somebody just happens to stumble acrost 'im."

"I guess so," Baker agreed, satisfied that he was in no danger.

Back in Tilden, Gid was grouching. "I've spent enough time in the doc's office," Gid said. "Not that the company and the food isn't good," he added, smiling at Anna. "But I'd just feel better in my own hotel room."

"That's probably not a bad idea," Will said. "And since the hotel has a restaurant, you won't even have to go anywhere for your meals. But how do you think you'll handle going up and down the stairs?"

"Piece of cake. And now that I mention it, I think I saw a piece of cake. Anna, is it about time to eat anyway?"

"When have you ever let the clock tell you whether or not it's time to eat?" Will asked, with a little laugh.

Anna shook her head as she headed to the kitchen.

Felton and Paxton were in the Four Aces Saloon in Oakville, Texas. They weren't generally known by sight in Oakville, and those who did recognize them, kept quiet because they profited by their relationship.

Felton was reading a copy of the *Tilden Free Press.*

"Did you read this?" Felton asked, showing Paxton the newspaper.

"Jess, you know I can't read."

"That son of a bitch O'Neal squealed like a pig to keep from bein' hanged. He's been sentenced to life in prison."

"Well, squealin' on us didn't do him that much good then, did it? It didn't do him no good at all. He's goin' to prison."

"But he ain't gettin' hung is he?"

"That's what you told me this here paper says."

"Well, then, there you go," Felton said. "We'll talk about it later. Here comes Scarborough," Felton said.

Ben Scarborough was the reason Felton and Paxton were in Oakville. The man approaching their table was a big man, at least six feet four inches tall, and well over two hundred pounds. The weight he packed was muscle, and if his size didn't frightened people, his face did. His nose had been cut off in a knife fight so that the only thing left was a scarred mass of flesh with two holes that resembled a pig's snout.

"So, you like my idea of hittin' the bank in Beeville, do you?" Scarborough asked, as he sat down, accepting Felton's invitation to join them at the table."

"Yeah, I do. It's far enough away that nobody's likely to recognize us when we ride into town, and the bank there is big enough to have a lot more money than we got from the bank in Pettus," Felton said.

"I'd be willin' to bet it's got as much money as that

coach you boys tried to rob," Scarborough said.

Felton laughed, a quiet, bitter laugh.

"What are you laughin' at?" Scarborough asked. "You don't think the bank will have that much money."

"It wouldn't have to have much to beat that stagecoach," Felton said. "I'm sure there warn't no money a' tall on that stage. I believe they just put that news out to trap us. It was a trick."

"Maybe so. But at least the bank ain't no trick," Scarborough said. "Banks always has money. So, when do you want to hit it?"

"I've got something else I want to do first," Felton said.

"What are you a sayin'?" Paxton asked.

"I'll let you know later. But right now, we need some more men to join up with us."

"I can come up with one for you, right now," Scarborough said.

"Who?"

"It's Ed Kildeer's younger brother, Jamie."

"Where is he?"

Scarborough pointed. "That's him, sittin' at that table over there. He's just waitin' for me to call 'im over."

"Damn, he ain't no more 'n a boy," Paxton said.

"Call 'im over here," Felton said.

"Jess, surely you ain't goin' to take on no boy, are you?" Paxton complained. "Hell, he's still wet behind the ears."

"Yeah, I'm goin' to take him on. He's probably pissed off enough about his brother gettin' killt, that he'd be willin' to do purt' near anythin' I asked him to do. And I've got a few ideas. Call 'im over here."

Scarborough held up his hand and signaled for Kildeer to come over to the table.

"You're Ed's younger brother?" Felton asked, when the boy came over.

"Yeah, I'm his only brother. That is, I was his only brother, before the Crocketts killt him."

"What's your name?"

"Jamie. Jamie Kildeer."

"Jamie, if I let you ride with us, are you willin' to do what I tell you to do, without 'ny questions?"

"Any chance we'll run across the Crockett brothers?"

"I imagine we'll meet up with the Crocketts, yeah."

Jamie grinned. "Then yeah, I'm willin' to do anythin' you tell me to do."

"All right, you can ride with us. Scarborough, can you come up with at least one more good man?"

"I'll start lookin'," Scarborough promised.

178

Chapter Nineteen

Sheriff McMurtry was having coffee and a sweet roll in the Morning Star Hotel dining room where he had come to meet with Will.

"I can't leave the town unprotected," Sheriff McMurtry said, "so Ward is going to have to stay back to keep an eye on things for me while I take O'Neal to Huntsville. I'd like to ask you to go with me, if you don't mind."

"I don't mind at all. I'll be glad to go with you," Will said. "When do you want to leave?"

"Two more days, Tuesday, right after dinner. We'll have to make camp that night."

"You haven't gone fancy on me, have you Ty?" Will asked. "When you say dinner, you're talking about the meal you eat in the middle of the day, right?"

Ty chuckled. "Yeah, of course I am. I've never figured out why anyone would want to call supper, dinner, anyway."

That night Will and Gid had supper in The Tinderbox Saloon. They invited the sisters, Millie Jean and Sara Sue, to have supper with them. They satisfied their obligation to the saloon by buying enough drinks for the two girls to pay for the time they were with them. The drinks were tea of course, but everyone understood that the percentage girls couldn't actually drink whiskey all day long.

"This is nice, isn't it?" Millie Jean asked. "Two sisters, sitting at the same table with two brothers."

"Yes," Sara Sue said. "It's too bad we had to all meet like this, though. I mean if we could have met before ... before," Sara Sue interrupted her sentence and took in the saloon with a wave of her hand.

Millie Jean reached over to lay her hand on her sister's hand. "Darlin' let's just be glad that we were able to meet two men as nice as Gid and Will. In our jobs, that isn't always the case."

"You're right," Sara Sue said.

The piano player started then and Gid took Millie's hand in his.

"How about a dance?" he asked.

"Oh, Gid, with your leg, do you really think you should?"

"You don't think I'm going to let a little bullet hole stop me from dancing with a pretty girl now, do you?" Gid asked with a smile.

Forty-six miles east of Will, Gid, and The Tinderbox in Tilden, Texas, Ben Scarborough stepped into the Bucket O' Blood Saloon in Pettus, Texas.

With a big smile on her face, one of the bar girls started toward the door to greet him, but when she saw the big man, with a pig snout as a nose, the smile left her face, and her eyes clouded over with fear as she turned away from him as quickly as she could.

Scarborough was used to such a reaction from women, so it didn't even bother him anymore. He had learned, in the years since his nose had been cut off, that if he had enough money, what he looked like didn't matter. He stepped up to the bar.

Scarborough had spent a few months in Pettus a couple of years earlier, and though he didn't have anyone in particular in mind to recruit for Felton's gang, he figured this was as good a place to start as anywhere.

"Ben Scarborough, isn't it?" the bartender asked, coming down to see what he wanted.

"Damn, how the hell were you able to remember me?" Scarborough asked with a sardonic laugh as he put his hand to his nose.

"Good question," the bartender replied. "Especially since, if you're at this job long enough, you all start looking alike."

The smile left Scarborough's face. "That ain't funny."

"Sorry, didn't mean no harm in it. Whiskey or beer?"

"I'll have a whiskey."

"Oh," Hazel said, taking a seat at Baker's table. "I've never seen such an ugly man in my entire life."

"Who you talkin' about?"

"That big man, standing at the bar. He ain't got no nose."

"What? No nose you say?" Baker asked, showing interest in her comment.

"I guess he's got one, but it . . . it's a horrible lookin' thing."

"Like a pig's snout?" Baker asked.

"Yes, yes, exactly like a pig's snout," Hazel said, agreeing with him.

"Ben Scarborough," Baker said.

"What?"

"The man standing at the bar is Ben Scarborough."

"You know him?"

"Yeah, he's a friend of mine."

Baker got up from the table and walked over to the bar. "Sam, Mr. Scarborough's drink is on me," he said.

Scarborough turned toward him.

"Well I'll be damn," Scarborough said with a smile, though the smile distorted his face even more. He stuck his hand out. "If it ain't . . ."

"Morris," Baker replied emphatically. "It's been a while, I wasn't sure you'd remember my name."

For just a second, Scarborough had a puzzled look on his face, then he realized that Baker didn't want his real name used.

"Bring your drink over to the table, we can catch up on things," Baker invited.

Hazel was still sitting at the table and when she looked up, she still wore a frightened expression on her face.

"Hazel, how about you go visit with some other folks and let me 'n my old friend here talk?"

"Yes," Hazel replied with obvious relief.

"What are you doing here?" Scarborough asked. "The last I heard, you were somewhere out in West Texas. Or was it New Mexico?"

"I was in West Texas," Baker said. "But I had to leave. It got a little uncomfortable for me there."

"How uncomfortable?"

"There are some dodgers out on me, but no likenesses, so I'm using the name Morris."

"Yeah, I wondered about that. Say, Mar . . . uh, Morris, are you looking for a job?"

"That depends upon what the job is," Baker replied.

"Do you remember Jess Felton?"

"Yes, I remember him. Why do you ask?"

"Jess's lookin' for another man to ride with us, and he sent me out to try and find someone for him. Are you interested?"

A wide smile spread across Baker's face. "Damn, Scarborough, you won't believe this, but findin' Felton's the very reason I come here."

When Gid awakened the next morning, there was blood on the bedsheets and on his leg.

He was sitting on the edge of the bed, looking at the blood-soaked bandage when Will came in through the door that led between their two rooms.

"You about ready for break . . ." Will started, then, seeing the bloody bandage, he stopped in mid-statement. "Damn, Gid, what happened?"

"I don't know, I woke up like this."

Will washed the blood from Gid's leg, then used the pillowcase as a bandage.

"All right, we need to get you back to the doc's office."

"I hope walking on it doesn't open it up again."

"You won't be walking on it."

"How else am I going to get there?"

"I'm going to go get the wheelchair."

Before leaving the hotel, Will stopped at the front desk.

"I'm afraid my brother just bled all over your sheets and I used a pillow case for a bandage." He gave the clerk five dollars. "This ought to take care of it."

The desk clerk smiled. "Indeed, it will, sir."

Five minutes later Will returned with the wheelchair. Leaving it at the foot of the stairs, he went up to get Gid, then helped him down the stairs.

"Oh, dear me, what happened?" the clerk asked.

"Just take it from me, you don't ever want to make my brother mad," Gid said.

"Oh my!"

Then the clerk saw the two of them laughing.

"I do believe you are having some fun with me," the clerk said.

"I've never had so much fun," Gid said as he dropped into the wheelchair.

"Let's get him up on the operating table and take a look at him," Dr. Burke said when Will pushed Gid into the doctor's office.

"Seems like almost every time I come in here, I have to take off my pants," Gid said, though he didn't resist.

"Who put this on?" Dr. Burke said, referring to the pillow case.

"I did," Will said.

"Under the circumstances, you did a good job."

Dr. Burke cut off the bloodied bandage so he could examine the bullet hole.

"I don't know how this opened up again. It's like you ran on it, or something."

"Danced?" Gid asked.

"Ah, yes, that would do it. But fortunately, it doesn't look too serious," Dr. Burke said as he inspected the wound. "It doesn't appear that you have any infection." He turned to retrieve some cotton and then soaked it in alcohol. After cleaning the bullet hole, he opened a cabinet and pulled out some gauze.

"I think you'd better stay here for a while. I need to keep an eye on you so you don't decide you can try and break a bucking horse."

"Aw, Doc, you know I wouldn't do a stupid thing like that," Gid said.

"And you don't think dancing is a stupid thing," Dr. Burke said as he began to bandage the wound.

"I'll leave my brother in your hands for a while," Will said. "And Gid, you make sure you do whatever the doctor says. If you wind up getting infection, you risk losing that leg, and if that happens, I can tell you you're too heavy for me to be carrying around. Do you understand? Nobody's teasing about this."

"I'll be the best patient Dr. Burke has ever had," Gid promised, contritely.

* * *

"Damn, I remember this place," Baker said as he and Scarborough approached the hideout. "This was Jess's mama's cabin. I should have thought of this place before."

"I didn't know it belonged to his mama," Scarborough said. "I just thought it was some place he run acrost."

"He brought me out here to show it to me oncet."

"You 'n Felton was friends, was you?"

"Yeah, we was oncet."

The two men took their horses to a lean-to then went into the cabin.

"I'll be damn," Felton said. "Martin Baker. I thought you was dead."

"They's lots of folks that would like for me to be dead," Baker said, as he laughed.

"What are you doing here?"

"I brung 'im," Scarborough said. "You said you was a' wantin' one more man. Me 'n Baker done a job together one time, 'n when I seen 'im in the Bucket O' Blood saloon, I asked him if he'd like to join us."

"Bucket O' Blood? Baker, what the hell was you doin' in Pettus? Last I heard of you, you was out in El Paso or some such place."

"Yeah, well, I was in West Texas, but I had to leave in a hurry. So I come back here, lookin' for you. We done pretty good together before; I figure we might be able to do it again."

"We will do it again," Felton said. "But I've got somethin' else to do first. I need to take care of some business with the Crockett brothers."

"Damn! Me too!" Scarborough said. "When are we goin' to do it?"

"I don't know what time it'll be, but it'll be done tomorrow."

"Tomorrow?"

"Yes."

Scarborough laughed. "Looks like I got here just in time."

Chapter Twenty

When Will stopped in to check on Gid later that morning, he was sitting at the table with Dr. Burke and Anna, enjoying a dinner of meatloaf, mashed potatoes, gravy, green beans, and freshly baked rolls.

"Will, won't you join us?" Anna asked as she rose to get a plate.

"Everything looks so good; don't I wish I could join you, but I can't. I just promised Ty I'd join him at The Iron Skillet. He and I will be taking O'Neal to Huntsville, and we'll need to make sure we have a plan in place."

"What's there to plan?" Gid asked. "You're taking a prisoner to Huntsville."

"Actually, we've decided we'll be going to Cotulla first, then catch a train to Huntsville."

"I don't like it," Gid said. "I wish I could go with you."

"I do too, Little Brother, but maybe if you don't do

anything dumb like dancing the fandango again, you'll be able to, soon."

"If you won't listen to your doctor, at least listen to your brother," Dr. Burke said.

"All right, all right," Gid said, raising his hands. "You've convinced me. I rest my leg until the wound is healed."

"Doc, Anna, take good care of him. I probably won't have time to check in on him again. Oh, and Dr. Burke, we've been paid the reward money for O'Neal and Kildeer, so keep a good record of what we owe you."

"I was going to charge the county," Dr. Burke said.

"I'm pretty sure we can do better than the county."

Dr. Burke laughed. "I expect you could at that. Thank you, Will, I appreciate it."

When Will stepped into The Iron Skillet, Sheriff McMurtry was already sitting at a table, and he gave a summoning wave toward Will.

"Chicken pot pie is the special today," Ty said when Will sat down. "I remember your mom used to make that a lot."

Will nodded. "It was one of Pa's favorites." Will chuckled. "I seem to recall that you liked it too, since you had dinner over at our house often enough."

"You mean like you and Gid, and my ma's cherry pie? Gid could eat half a pie all by himself. Ma always made an extra pie if she knew Gid would be there. She had to, so the rest of us could have even a little bit."

"The boy does love to eat," Will agreed with a little laugh.

"How's he doing? Is his leg healing?"

"He was doing just fine until last night," Will said. "He got a little rambunctious with his dancing, and somehow that opened up everything again. He woke up with it bleeding this morning, and I had to take him back to Doctor Burke's office."

"I'll say this. He's in good hands, and you can call it an office, but it's damn near a hospital. Dr. Burke has been very good for this town."

"He's been very good for Gid. Actually, Anna has been good for Gid. I've no doubt but that he would have bled to death before we could get him back here, if it hadn't been for her."

"She's a fine young lady," Ty said. He chuckled. "And if you don't believe me, you can ask Ward."

"He does seem to be taken with her," Will said.

"He's asked me to be his best man."

"Oh, so he and Anna are getting married."

"I'm sure they will." Ty laughed. "The thing is, he's asked me to be his best man, but he hasn't asked Anna to be his wife yet."

Will chuckled. "I may be mistaken, but it seems to me

like if you are going to ask someone to be your best man, you should at least have a wedding in mind."

"Oh, I've no doubt but that's what he has in mind. He just hasn't worked up the courage to talk to Anna about it. Everyone who knows them, knows that she would accept his proposal in a heartbeat."

"Ward seems like a pretty good deputy," Will said.

"Best I ever had. He's got the courage and the toughness, but he has something more, something that might be even more important to the job. Ward is a very smart young man, and I don't mean just because he has two years of college. He's just naturally smart. I've been figuring on retiring in another couple of years, and when I do, I'm going to support Ward for Sheriff."

"Retire? Why, you're no older than I am. What do you mean, retire?" Will asked.

"I didn't mean retire as in doing nothing. I just mean retire from being sheriff. Fred Clark is about ready to sell out his business, and he said he'd make me a good deal on buying his half of his freighting operation. I might ask Lucy to marry me then. Never figured it was fair to ask someone to marry a sheriff and put up with all a sheriff has to go through."

"Lucy?"

"Lucy McPheters, she's a widow woman 'bout my same age. And I think she'd marry me in a minute if I'd ask."

"Sounds like you have everything all planned."

"What about you and Gid? Do you think you boys will ever settle down?"

"I don't know," Will said. "There's nobody on the horizon for either one of us."

"It's too bad that . . ." Ty started, but he paused in mid-sentence.

"Gid and Katie, I know," Will said. "Sherman might have been a Yankee general, but when he said, 'War is hell', I sure agree with him. It killed half a million, and no doubt changed the lives of millions more."

The next job Felton had planned, was to rob the bank in Beeville. It was Felton's intention to use Jamie Kildeer to scout out the bank and the law in Beeville and bring him the information he could use to plan the bank robbery. Jamie had never been to Beeville and had never been arrested so there was no danger in sending him in to scout the town. But he had something else that he wanted to take care of first, so he sent Jamie to Tilden to get information for him.

The main reason Felton had been willing to take Jamie into his gang was because he realized that Jamie's youth might actually be an advantage, giving him the anonymity that would allow him to find out information without arousing suspicion, especially the information he wanted pertaining to when O'Neal was to be taken to Huntsville and the route the sheriff would take.

Jamie's first stop in Tilden was The Iron Skillet Restaurant, because he wanted something beyond the fare he and the others had been eating at the cabin. As it happened, while he was in The Iron Skillet, he found himself sitting at the table next to the sheriff and Will Crockett. He was well positioned, close enough to overhear everything Will and Ty were saying. And if they would happen to glance over toward him, they wouldn't see anything any more sinister than a young man eating a piece of apple pie and drinking a glass of milk. But he was there, specifically to gather information for Jess Felton. Jamie looked over at Will, without obviously staring.

You're the son of a bitch that killt my brother, he thought.

"All right, we are agreed," Ty said. "We'll meet here for dinner tomorrow, then take our prisoner to Huntsville."

"By way of the train at Cotulla," Will said with a smile. "I'd hate to have to ride all the way to Huntsville while also keeping an eye on O'Neal."

Saying goodbye to Ty, Will went back to the doctor's office to check on Gid. He was sitting at a table playing two-hand poker with Anna.

"You'd better keep an eye on him, Anna. He cheats," Will warned.

"Huh, uh, I only cheat at solitaire," Gid replied. "And that doesn't count, because I only cheat myself. Anyway, if I'm cheating, why do I owe Anna thirty-five cents?"

"I don't know. Maybe it's because you aren't all that good at cheating," Will said with a little laugh.

"Have you got everything lined up for transporting O'Neal to prison tomorrow?" Gid asked.

"As far as I know, we have. And I expect to be back within five days."

"I should be feeling chipper then," Gid said. "Then we can go after Felton and Paxton."

"Yeah, well, I don't want to get you out too fast. You saw what happened the other night."

"I'll be more careful this time," Gid said. "I mean, come on, Will, you don't expect me to just sit around and twiddle my thumbs, do you?"

"No, I expect you to get better, so I won't have to do all the work."

* * *

Felton, Baker, Paxton and Scarborough had camped no more than ten miles from Tilden so that Jamie didn't have to go the twenty-five miles back to the cabin to find them.

"They'll be moving O'Neal tomorrow afternoon," Jamie said, helping himself to a cup of coffee from the campfire.

"That's good to know," Felton said. "That means we can take care of business tomorrow."

"I thought we were going to hit the bank tomorrow," Scarborough said.

"The bank will still be there, but if we don't do this tomorrow, O'Neal will already be in prison," Felton said.

"You must think a lot of that guy to put cuttin' him loose ahead of robbin' the bank," Scarborough said.

"Yeah," Felton said, without further elaboration. "You would think so, wouldn't you?" He looked over toward Jamie. "So they're taking him to Cotulla, right?"

"That's what they said."

Felton nodded. "We'll spend the night here. You done good, boy."

Jamie beamed with pride.

That evening, Will stopped by The Tinderbox Saloon to have a nightcap. He planned to have only one beer before going back to his room and going to bed. If Gid had been with him, he might have had two, or three beers, and might have even gotten into a poker game. But Gid wasn't with him, and he had a full day planned for tomorrow.

"How's Gid doing?"

Turning in response to a woman's voice, Will saw Millie Jean standing there.

"Hello, Darlin'," Will said.

"When Sheriff McMurtry was in here earlier, he said Gid had to go back to see the doctor," Millie said, a genuine sense of concern in her voice. "It's because of me, isn't it? It's because I danced with him."

"Don't be blaming yourself, Millie Jean. If you hadn't danced with him, he would have had a few more beers, and then that big lummox would have gotten out onto that floor and danced by himself. He opened the wound again, but the doctor says it isn't anything serious. He'll be just fine."

"Good," Millie Jean said. "I . . . well, him being so nice to me 'n all, I wouldn't want to see anything happen to him."

"Here, have a drink with me," Will said.

"Thanks," Millie Jean replied with a smile.

"I'll be seeing Gid in the morning, I'll tell him you asked about him."

"Thank you. I . . . uh, don't get me wrong, I know there's nothing, uh, I mean . . . I'm just asking as a friend, is all."

Will studied Millie Jean for a moment. The expression on her face reflected the heartbreak of her circumstances. She had been forced into this life because she had defended her sister, and her eyes told the story of having a normal life forever snatched from her.

Will put his hand, lightly, on Millie's shoulder. "Millie Jean, Gid is proud, and I am too, to call you our friend."

Millie's eyes filled with tears, and she blinked several times. "I, uh, I have to go," she said.

Will watched her leave the saloon floor.

"Somehow you, and your brother have gotten to Millie, and her sister too," Clyde said, coming over to pick up Millie's empty glass.

"Clyde, when we buy a drink for one of these girls, how much do they get from each drink?"

"They get half, and the saloon gets half," Clyde answered.

Will took out fifty dollars and handed it to Clyde. "Clyde, here's fifty dollars' worth of drinks. I would appreciate it, if you would take the saloon cut out of this and divide the rest of the money up between Millie Jean and her sister."

"You're a good man, Will Crockett," Clyde said. "The saloon can get along without its cut."

Leaving the saloon, Will walked down to the jail. Ty wasn't there, but Ward was.

"Good evening, Will," Ward said when Will stepped inside. "Anything I can do for you?"

"No, I'm about to go back to the hotel, but I thought I might check in on our prisoner before I turn in for the night."

"Sure, go on back."

O'Neal was sitting on his bunk with his knees drawn up before him, and his hands wrapped around his legs. There was no lantern in the cell, but the common area between the cells was brightly illuminated.

"Ready for your trip tomorrow?" Will asked with a grin.

"I wouldn't be so cocksure you're going to get me there," O'Neal said.

"Oh? And why not?"

"I've got friends."

"You mean friends like Jess Felton?"

"Yeah, friends like Jess Felton. Like I said, I wouldn't count on you getting me there, if I were you. Felton, Paxton, and by now I'm sure he's rounded up some others to replace me 'n Kildeer. There's no way he's goin' to let you get me to prison."

Will chuckled, then turned to leave. "I'll see you tomorrow, O'Neal."

Chapter Twenty-one

Felton, Paxton, Scarborough, and Jamie Kildeer were sitting around a campfire, eating the rabbit they had killed for their supper.

"We'll camp here tonight," Felton said. "This'll put us in position to stop McMurtry and Crockett when they come through here taking O'Neal to prison."

"I still don't see no reason why we're doin' this," Scarborough said.

"You have a problem with it?" Felton asked.

"Yeah, I've got a problem. O'Neal took his chances just like everyone else did. At least he warn't killt, 'n he ain't a' gonna be hung. I say we forget about rescuin' him. There ain't no money in it. But there is money in the bank in Beeville, and that's what we need to be thinkin' about."

"I *am* thinking about it," Felton said. "But we do this first."

Scarborough gave sort of a disgusting, grunting sound.

"Scarborough, if you don't want to ride with the rest of us, you're certainly free to go out on your own."

"No, now, there ain't no need for nothin' like that. I mean if you want to rescue O'Neal, why, I reckon we could prob'ly use another man."

"Yeah," Felton said. Felton and Paxton exchanged a glance that neither Scarborough, nor any of the others noticed.

"I told you that Crockett is comin' with the sheriff," Jamie said. "We're goin' to kill 'im, aren't we? Crockett, I mean. He's the son of a bitch that killt my brother."

"We'll take care of Crockett," Felton promised.

"Good. I'm countin' on you to do just that."

While Felton and the others were gathered around the campfire, Ty was in Tilden, standing at the corner of Ash and Congress Street. He had chosen this particular address, because this was the location of the house where Lucy McPheters lived. Lucy had moved to Tilden six months ago, and since moving she and Ty had been keeping company with one another until it developed into actual courting.

Ty had told Will that he thought Lucy would marry him in a minute if he would ask.

He was about to find out.

He had been thinking about it for some time now and had made the decision that he was going to ask her this evening. But now that he was here, standing out in front of her house, he wasn't sure that he had the courage to do it.

"Come on, Ty," he said aloud. "You've faced down men who were shooting at you. How can you be afraid of a sweet woman like Lucy?"

To Ty's surprise, the front door opened.

"Ty, what in the world are you doing just standing out there?" Lucy called out to him. "Aren't you going to come in?"

"Yes, I just, uh . . . yes, I'm coming in."

"I was wondering what time you would get here this evening. I made a cherry pie just for you. I know it won't be as good as you say your mama's cherry pie was, but any cherry pie is good. How about a piece of pie now, and a cup of freshly made coffee?" Luci invited.

"That sounds great," Ty said, following Lucy into the kitchen.

"Have a seat, I'll serve you," Lucy said, pointing to the kitchen table.

"You'll be taking the prisoner tomorrow?" Lucy asked as she cut the pie.

"Yes. I expect I'll be gone about five days or so."

"Ty, please be careful."

"There's nothing to worry about. Transporting a prisoner is pretty routine, and of course I'll have Will Crockett with me."

"You said you and Will have been friends for a long time?"

"Yes, ever since we were kids. Our farms were adjoining."

"I'm glad he'll be with you. I can't help but worry a little. Actually, I worry about you all the time."

"That brings up something I want to talk to you about," Ty said. "What would you say, if I promised you, you'd never have to worry about me again?"

"I think that would be wonderful, but how can you make such a promise?"

"I can make it, because as soon as I get back from this trip, I'm buying Fred Clark's half of Clark and Hopkins. I'm going to take off my badge and become a freight dealer."

"Oh, I think that is a wonderful idea," Lucy replied with a broad smile.

"I'm glad you like it. Now I'm going to ask you something else."

"Yes, I'll marry you," Lucy said.

"What?"

"That is what you were going to ask, isn't it? If I would marry you?"

"Doggone it, and here I had a little speech all worked out, too."

"You can still give your little speech," Lucy said with a teasing smile.

"Nah, I'll just come out and say it. And I'm not nervous about it, now that I know your answer. Lucy, will you marry me?"

"Let me think about it."

"What?" Ty replied to her unexpected response.

Lucy laughed. "Yes, I'll marry you."

"Good. Let's get married as soon as I get back."

"As soon as you get back," Lucy said, sealing the bargain with a kiss. "When are you leaving?"

"Tomorrow afternoon."

"Come by for lunch tomorrow before you go," Lucy invited.

"I'd be glad to."

Anna had invited Will to Dr. Burke's office for lunch the next day, so he could eat with Gid before he left on his trip.

"Thanks for the invitation," Will said as he was led into the dining room where Gid was waiting at the table.

"Think nothing of it," Anna replied with a cheerful little smile. "I just thought you might enjoy your last meal with your brother."

204

"Whoa," Will said with a little laugh. "Let's not be so intent on making this my *last* meal."

Anna laughed as well, this time a nervous little laugh. "Well, I didn't actually mean it that way," she said. "I mean nothing like a real last meal."

Now, Gid laughed. "He's teasing you, Anna."

The table was set, and Will, Gid, Anna, and Dr. Burke enjoyed a meal of fried chicken, mashed potatoes and gravy, and a fried peach pie for dessert.

"What time are you leaving?" Gid asked when they were finished with their dinner.

"I think Ty wants to get started about one o'clock."

"Will?"

"Yes."

"I don't have a good feeling about this," Gid said.

"What do you mean?" Will asked.

"I don't know. It's just that you and I always take care of one another, and this time you'll be by yourself."

"I'm not going to be by myself," Will said. "Ty is the closest thing we have for a brother besides each another."

"I know, you're right. It just . . .well, be careful, will you?"

"You can count on it, Gid."

* * *

"Cabbage, fried taters, 'n bacon?" O'Neal said, complaining about the plate of food that was passed through the access slit in the cell bars. "Ain't we supposed to get our choice for the last meal?"

"That's only if you are about to be executed," Ward replied.

"Yeah, well, seems to me like you ought to get your choice just before you get put in prison for life, too."

"Take it up with the warden when you get to Huntsville," Ward suggested. "Maybe he'll see it your way."

"Yeah, well it'll be too late then, won't it?" O'Neal complained. "I'll already be in prison."

"You may have a point there," Ward said, chuckling as he returned to the front of the office to take his own meal, which was exactly the same thing as had been provided for his prisoner.

Ward was just finishing his lunch when Ty came into the office, having taken his dinner with Lucy.

"How did your dinner go with Mrs. McPheters?" Ward asked, topping off his meal with a cup of coffee.

"Fine," Ty said, with a broad smile. "But it won't be Mrs. McPheters much longer."

"You asked her."

"I did, and she said yes."

"Congratulations, Ty," Ward said, shaking Ty's hand.

When Will returned to the office, Ty shared with him the news of his engagement. Congratulations were exchanged, along with some teasing and spirited conversation. Finally, Ty got to the business at hand.

"Will, is your horse out front?" Ty asked.

"It's there."

"I'll go get our prisoner," Ty said, taking the cell key down from the hook on the wall.

"Ty, I got your horse and O'Neal's horse ready to go too. They're out back, I'll bring them around while you're getting O'Neal," Ward said.

"All right, thanks," Ty said. He walked into the back, to the jail cells. O'Neal was sitting in the single chair, with his legs stretched out so that his feet were on the bed.

"All right, O'Neal, on your feet, let's go," Ty ordered. "Stick your hands through the bars."

O'Neal did so.

"Not like that, you idiot, you have a bar between your hands. Stick them both through the same space.

"You didn't say anything about sticking both hands through the same space."

"Well, if you had the common sense of a cockroach, I wouldn't have had to tell you."

Ty attached handcuffs, then, opening the door, led the cuffed O'Neal to the front of the office.

"All right, Ward," Ty said as he reached for his hat.

"The town is in your hands.

"It'll be here when you get back," Ward said. "Lucy McPheters will be, too," he added with a smile.

Chapter Twenty-two

Felton, Baker, Paxton, Scarborough and Jamie Kildeer, were waiting alongside the road that ran from Tilden to Cotulla, very close to where they had spent the night. It was the perfect place for an ambush because of the very sharp turn in the road, and a rather substantial gathering of very large rocks which would supply not only concealment, but cover, in the event something went wrong and they were to get into a shooting match.

"Are you sure they'll be coming this way?" Scarborough asked.

"You know any other way to get from Tilden to Cotulla?" Felton asked.

"No, this is the Cotulla road, all right," Scarborough said.

"Then this is where we'll wait."

"I guess I can see rescuing O'Neal," Scarborough

finally conceded. "I mean, if I was the one that was bein' took to prison, I'd appreciate bein' rescued."

"Would you now?" Felton asked in a dismissive voice.

"When they get here, I want to be the one that kills Will Crockett," Jamie said. "He's the son of a bitch that killt my brother, 'n I aim to get him for that."

"We ain't goin' to kill 'im, I got other plans for 'im," Felton said.

"I want the son of a bitch dead," Jamie said again.

"And I said I have other plans for him, so you'll either do it the way I say, or you can go off on your own."

"We ain't goin' to just rescue O'Neal and let Crockett go, are we?" Jamie asked.

"It's like I said, I've got plans of my own," Felton replied.

"Well, don't you think the rest of us might ought to know what them plans is?" Scarborough asked.

"It's best not to let too many people know what I got in mind," Felton said. "That way there's less chance of making a mistake. Paxton knows, 'n that's all that needs to know for now."

"Yeah, well I hope your plans do include us takin' the money from the bank over in Beeville. They do, don't they?" Baker asked.

"Oh, yes, indeed they do," Felton said. "And trust me, after we take care of this here little bit of business, robbin' that bank is goin' to be a whole lot easier."

"I wonder how much money they've got 'n that bank?" Jamie asked.

"What do you care, kid?" Paxton teased. "It'll more 'n likely be more money 'n you've ever had in your whole life, all put together."

"Well, hell, Paxton, that don't mean nothin'," Scarborough teased. "Twenty dollars would more 'n likely be more 'n the boy's ever had in his life."

Ward had walked down to the doctor's office where he, Anna, and Gid were on the front porch so they could watch Will, Ty, and their prisoner pass by. Ward had told Lucy to come as well, and when she arrived, he brought enough chairs out front so all of them would have a place to sit.

"Well now, would you just look at us," Gid said.

"What is it?" Ward asked.

"With all of us sittin' in chairs like this, you'd think we were getting ready to watch a horse race," Gid said.

"Yeah, I guess it does look like that," Ward agreed.

"Lucy, Will told us the sheriff has asked you to marry him. I'm real happy for you," Anna said.

"Oh, thank you. Ty made me a very happy woman, last night." She chuckled. "It took him long enough in getting around to doing it. I think he was ready to ask me a month ago, but it took him a while to get up his courage."

"I can believe that," Gid said. "It always has taken Ty a long time to make up his mind about something. I remember, he couldn't make up his mind about Cindy ... did he want her or not, until finally he decided he did want her but by then, she was with somebody else."

"Cindy?" Lucy asked. "He's never told me about her. Did she marry someone else?"

"What?" Gid asked, then he laughed. "Oh, no, I'm sorry I didn't make myself clearer. Cindy was a horse Ty almost bought."

The others laughed as well.

"Lucy, if you need any help with your wedding, I'd be glad to help out," Anna said.

"Thanks, Anna. I'd be happy to have your help. I know there'll be lots to do, since Ty has so many friends that he'll want to come to the wedding. Lots of baking, I'm afraid."

As Will and Ty were escorting their prisoner, Ty was sharing his plans about buying half of the freight yard.

"Soon as I buy Fred Clark out, I'm goin' to talk Elmer Hopkins into us puttin' another warehouse in, over in Los Lomas. We can get Dan Evans to run it, he's a good man."

"What does Lucy think about you giving up being a sheriff to go into the freighting business?" Will asked.

"I expect this is going to work out really well," Ty said.

"First of all, Lucy's always been a little scared about me being a sheriff, and you can't blame her, her husband gettin' himself killed while he was with the Texas Rangers. I don't blame her for not wanting to have to go through anything like that, again.

"And Fred has done really well with the business, which is likely to keep on making money for at least thirty or forty more years, especially if we add another warehouse."

"I think you've made a pretty wise decision, Ty," Will replied. "It will certainly provide you with a lucrative future."

O'Neal laughed, a mocking laugh. "Future." He laughed again. "You folks are talking about a future, as iffen you're goin' to have one. Felton ain't even a' goin' to allow you to get me to Cotulla, let alone Huntsville."

Jamie Kildeer, who had been posted as a lookout, about a quarter of a mile east of where Felton and the others were waiting, came running back.

"They're on their way!" he said excitedly, breathing hard from the run.

"How far are they?" Felton asked.

"Oh, not more 'n a mile I'd say."

"All right, they'll be here in ten minutes or so. Ever' one get ready," Felton ordered.

213

Will, Ty, and O'Neal had come about ten miles since leaving Tilden, and so far, it had been an easy transfer. O'Neal had given them no trouble, and except for a few sarcastic comments, had been mostly silent for the ride.

The road in front of them made a sharp turn to the right. This was the first such turn since they had left Tilden. The turn was so sharp that it left a blind spot just in front of them, and Will grew a little uneasy about it.

Will's apprehension was justified when, no more than a moment later, five armed men appeared in front of them, spread all the way across the road.

"Put your hands up!" the leader of the men called. Will recognized him as one of the men he and Gid had encountered during the stagecoach hold up, so he surmised it must be Jess Felton.

Ty put his hands up, and Will had no choice but to do the same.

"Get down offen your horses," Felton ordered.

Will and Ty dismounted.

"Ha!" O'Neal shouted happily. "I knew you boys would come get me, I been tellin' 'em you was goin' to."

"Baker?" Will said, surprised to see him here. "Baker, you're with them?"

"Yeah," Baker said with a wide grin. "I'm what you might call resourceful."

"Both of you, use your thumb and forefinger to take your pistols out of your holsters, 'n drop 'em on the ground."

Will and Ty complied.

"Get over here, O'Neal," Felton said.

"Tell me, McMurtry, just what you goin' to say to the warden at the state prison when I don't show up? You goin' to tell 'im that you couldn't hold on to your prisoner?" O'Neal taunted as he guided his horse over to join Felton and the others. "Hey, Felton, the sheriff's got the key to these handcuffs. Why don't you get 'em, so's you can take 'em off me? My wrists is beginnin' to get sore."

"In due time," Felton replied. "Paxton, toss the rope over that tree limb."

That was when Will saw a rope with a noose at one end, while the other end was tied off.

"Ha, 'n you fellas was wantin' to hang me," O'Neal taunted. "Looks to me like you're the ones that's fixin' to get hung."

Will got a weak feeling in the pit of his stomach. The possibility of dying in a gunfight had always been near, but he had never considered being hanged.

"Well now, Sheriff Ty McMurtry and Mr. Will Crockett," O'Neal taunted. "What do you have to say now?"

To the shock of Will, the sheriff, and especially to O'Neal, Felton and Paxton turned their guns toward

O'Neal, while the remaining three held their guns steady on Will and the sheriff.

"Get over here, O'Neal," Felton ordered.

"What's goin' on here?" O'Neal asked.

When O'Neal was in position, Paxton dropped the loop around his neck.

"Hey, hold on here, what the hell are . . ." that was as far as O'Neal got before his horse was slapped out from under him. O'Neal gasped and struggled, holding his handcuffed hands up to the rope around his neck.

"That's for squealin' on Paxton 'n me, you double-crossin' son of a bitch," Felton told the struggling O'Neal.

O'Neal made insensible gargling sounds, as he kicked and twisted his body in a desperate and fruitless attempt to fight against the hanging, then he grew still, except for the lazy swinging of his dead body.

"Scarborough, you step up behind 'em, 'n keep an eye on' em. Kildeer, you go empty their pockets," Felton said.

"Yeah," Jamie said, as he reached his hand down into Will's pocket. "Crockett, my name is Kildeer. Jamie Kildeer. The Kildeer you killt was my brother, Eddie."

Although Will and Gid had drawn five hundred dollars reward money for the two Felton men they had accounted for, after giving the Sanders sisters the fifty dollars, he had brought less than twenty dollars for this trip. Sheriff McMurtry had brought a little more because he would have been buying the train tickets for the three of them when they reached Cotulla.

"That's it? That's all the money you two are carrying?" Felton asked when Jamie handed over the money.

"What about this here pocket knife," Jamie Kildeer said. "It looks like a pretty good knife, 'n I aim to keep it."

"Go ahead, kid, you can keep it. The sheriff won't be havin' no need for it."

Felton nodded at Scarborough, and Scarborough brought the butt of his gun down on top of Will's head, knocking him out.

"What did you do that for? You could have killed him," McMurtry complained.

"I didn't intend to kill him," Felton said. He walked over and picked up Will's gun. "I intend to kill you."

Without another word, Felton pulled the trigger on the gun he was holding.

Sheriff Ty McMurtry, Will and Gid's childhood friend, brother of the woman Gid had once loved, fell dead, killed by a bullet from Will's gun.

"Now, I aim to kill this son of a bitch!" Kildeer said, pointing his pistol at the unconscious Will's head.

"No, you ain't a' goin' to kill 'im," Felton said.

"What? Why the hell can't I kill him?"

"On account of 'cause I got somethin' else in mind," Felton said.

Felton leaned over and put Will's gun in his hand, then he walked back to his horse and took out a bottle of whiskey. He took one swallow, then held the bottle out.

"Boy, come here 'n take this whiskey."

"You know I don't drink, Mr. Felton," Jamie replied.

"Didn't say nothin', 'bout drinkin'," Felton said. "That's why I'm choosin' you. Iffen I was to give this bottle to any of the other galoots, they'd more 'n likely drink too much of it before they did what I want done with it. I want you to empty this bottle on Crockett."

"Come on, Jess, that's a pure dee waste o' good whiskey," Paxton complained.

"No it ain't. When they find 'em here, they're goin' to think that Crockett killed the sheriff, hung O'Neal, then got drunk to celebrate 'n passed out."

Jamie Kildeer did as he was told and started to throw the bottle away.

"No, don't throw it away. Drop it right there alongside 'im."

Jamie dropped the bottle.

"All right, boys, let's get out of here," Felton ordered.

Chapter Twenty-three

When Will came to, he wasn't quite sure what had happened to him. He saw O'Neal's body hanging from the tree limb, and he remembered that.

"Ty, what happened here? Was I . . ." That was when Will saw the sheriff lying on the ground.

"Ty!" Will called, then realizing that he was holding his gun, he pushed it down into his holster and hurried over to his friend, thinking they must have knocked him out as well.

"Ty, Ty, come out of it," Will said, then, leaning down to turn him over, he saw the bullet wound right over his heart.

"Ty!" he said. "No, damn!"

As Will stood there, looking down at the body of his friend, he heard horses approaching, and looking up toward them he saw two men, both wearing badges.

"I'm Deputy U.S. Marshal Vernon Crawford, this is Deputy U.S. Marshal Emmet Osborne. Who are you?" Crawford asked, as he dismounted.

"I'm Will Crockett," Will said. He pointed to the body on the ground. "That's Sheriff Ty McMurtry, and he deputized me to help him get that man," he pointed to O'Neal's body, hanging still and lifeless from the tree, "to prison."

"I know Sheriff McMurtry, and I've heard of you." Crawford pulled his pistol and pointed it at Will. "Hand over your pistol."

"What? Look here, Marshal, you don't think I did this, do you?"

"I said hand over your pistol. I'm not going to ask again."

Will pulled his pistol and handed it, butt first, to the marshal. Crawford spun the cylinder and saw the dimple the firing pin had put on one of the cartridges.

"Tell me, Crockett, did you get drunk before, or after you murdered the sheriff?"

"What? What are you talking about?"

"Sheriff McMurtry is dead, his pistol is in his holster. You are alive, and one bullet in your gun has been fired. Also, you reek of whiskey."

"They must have poured it on me."

"Who must have poured it on you?"

"Felton and his gang. That must have been when they murdered Ty."

"Must have been? You mean you didn't see it?"

"I was knocked out," Will said. "And just what makes you think I would kill Ty, anyway? What reason would I have for doing something like that?"

"We read about you in the newspaper, Crockett, and how you were upset because O'Neal wasn't sentenced to hang. I figure you wormed your way into transporting the prisoner with Sheriff McMurtry, and when he wouldn't go along with what you had in mind, you killed him, then hung O'Neal yourself."

"I did not kill Ty McMurtry, and I did not hang Paddy O'Neal."

"He hung himself, I suppose."

"No, he was hanged by Felton and his men."

"And just why would Felton hang one of his own men?"

"He said it was because O'Neal turned state's evidence on him. Well, he didn't put it that way, I doubt Felton has ever even heard the term. He said it was because O'Neal squealed on him."

"You're under arrest, Will Crockett. We're taking you back to Tilden to be tried for the murder of Sheriff McMurtry and Paddy O'Neal. And yes, even though he was a prisoner, hanging him like you did, without authorization of the court, is murder."

"You're making a big mistake," Will said.

"No, you're the one making the mis . . ." that was as far as Crawford got before Will took him down with an unexpected right cross.

"What the . . .?" Osborne shouted, when he saw his fellow Marshal on the ground, and Crawford's pistol in Will's hand.

"Hand over your pistol," Will ordered, even as he was retrieving his own gun from Crawford, who, groggily, was just getting up.

"Bring your two horses over to me."

Osborne brought the two horses over to Will and handed the reins to him.

"Both of you, get over there and lie down on your stomachs."

"Why the hell should we do that?" Crawford demanded.

Will shot two times, the shots coming so close together that it sounded like one shot. Both Crawford and Osborne felt their hats knocked off their heads.

"Because I told you to," Will said.

As the two marshals lay face down, Will mounted his horse and, still holding onto the reins, of the U.S. Marshals' horses rode off. The horse O'Neal had been riding was long gone, and the horse Sheriff McMurtry had been riding stood over the sheriff's body, looking down at him as if mourning his death.

222

Will's original thought was to return to Tilden, but he knew that the marshals would go there first and report him as a fugitive. He let the marshals' horses go, then left the road, and found a coulee deep enough to keep him from being seen from the road.

Crawford and Osbourne were deciding whether or not they would ride double on the sheriff's horse when, to their surprise, their horses came trotting back.

"Good, now we can go after the son of a bitch," Osbourne said.

"No, first we need to get the sheriff's body back to Tilden," Crawford said. "Anyway, that's probably the best place to start searching for Crockett."

When Crawford and Osborne rode into Tilden, leading a third horse, the citizens of Tilden noticed immediately that a body was draped over the horse. It wasn't until then that one sharp-eyed observer recognized the body.

"Oh, God in Heaven! That's Sheriff McMurtry!"

Once he was pointed out, others recognized the sheriff as well, and they started following the grim procession until it stopped in front of the sheriff's office.

Not until the two riders dismounted in front of the sheriff's office did people notice the stars they wore on their vest.

"That's Sheriff McMurtry," one of the citizens of the town said to Marshal Crawford. "What happened?"

Neither marshal replied to the questions but went into the sheriff's office where they found Deputy Haller sweeping the floor. He looked up when he saw the marshals enter.

"Hello, Marshal Crawford, Marshal Osborn. If you're looking for Ty, I mean, the sheriff, he isn't here," Ward said.

"You mean you didn't see us riding into town?" Crawford asked.

"No, I've been cleaning up in here. What's up?"

"We have Sheriff McMurtry draped across his horse, out front."

"What?" Ward Haller literally shouted the word. "Why? I mean, what happened?"

"Will Crockett murdered him, that's what happened," Osborn said.

Ward shook his head. "No, I don't believe that. I don't believe Will Crockett is the one that killed him."

"And why don't you believe it?"

"Because Will and the sheriff have been friends since both of them were children. They were practically raised together."

"Crockett and the sheriff were taking a prisoner to Huntsville?" Osborn asked.

"Yes. Well, to Cotulla. They were going to catch the train there."

"They never made it," Osborn said. "About ten miles from here, you'll find O'Neal hanging from a tree. Apparently, Crockett wanted to hang O'Neal, and when the sheriff protested, Crockett shot 'im."

"I still don't believe it," Haller said.

"Well, deputy, you had better believe it, because you are now the acting sheriff, and it will be your responsibility to arrest him, if he shows his face in Tilden, that is."

"Yes, well, the first thing I'm going to do is take care of Sheriff McMurtry."

"He's not the sheriff anymore," Osborn said. "He's just a stiff, 'n he was killed by Will Crockett."

Fifteen minutes later, Sheriff McMurtry's body was lying on the embalming table at Welsh's Undertaking Establishment.

"The county will pay for Ty's funeral," Ward said. "But I want you to do more than that. I want a first-class funeral for him, and I'll make up the difference between what the county will pay, and what you will charge."

Lonnie Welsh nodded. "You don't need to worry about that, Deputy. Trust me, we'll give him a fine send-off."

"Now comes the worst part," Ward said.

"What's that?" Welsh asked.

"I have to go talk to Lucy McPheters."

Ward was almost certain that Lucy already knew about it, news had spread through town like wildfire. But he owed it to Ty, and to Lucy, to personally give her the news.

He was going to ask Anna to go with him.

Chapter Twenty-four

"Hello, Ward, Gid and I were about to have a cup of coffee. You're just in time," Anna said, greeting Ward with a welcoming smile.

"Thanks," Ward said, following Anna back into the kitchen. Gid was sitting at the kitchen table.

"Hello, Ward," Gid greeted.

Ward joined them at the table and waited as Anna poured the coffee for him, then he lifted his cup and studied the two as he drank.

"What is it, Ward? Why are you looking like that?"

Ward lowered his cup.

"Ty's dead," Ward said.

"What?" Anna and Gid said, simultaneously.

"What happened?" Gid asked.

Ward studied Gid for a long moment, without replying.

"Oh, Ward, that's awful. But you didn't answer Gid's

question. What happened?"

"He was murdered."

"What about Will? Is he all right?" Gid asked, anxiously.

"I don't know," Ward answered.

"You don't know? Well, where is he?"

"I don't know that, either."

"Ward, what's going on here?" Gid asked. "There's something you aren't telling us."

Ward set his cup down, took a deep breath, then let out a long sigh.

"Gid, they're saying that Will killed Ty."

"What? That's crazy! Who is saying that?"

Ward told about the two marshals who had brought Ty's body into town.

"Where are they? I'd like to talk to them," Gid said.

"They're down at the sheriff's office. I haven't told them about you."

Gid reached for his crutch.

"Take me down there."

"Anna, I'll take Gid down to talk to the marshals, but then I need to go see Lucy. I'm dreading that. Would you go with me?"

"Of course, I will go."

When Gid and Ward stepped into the sheriff's office, one of the marshals was sitting behind Ty's desk, while the other was perusing the wanted posters that were tacked to the wall.

"Did you get everything taken care of with the undertaker?" Marshal Crawford asked.

"Yes," Ward replied.

"Who's this?" Marshal Osborne asked.

"Crockett," Gid replied. "Gid Crockett."

"Crockett? Are you related to the man who killed the sheriff?"

"No," Gid said. "Will Crockett is my brother; I have no idea who killed Ty. But I'm sure I'm not related to him."

"You call the sheriff Ty?"

"Why not? We have known each other since we were ten years old."

"Yes, that's what you said about Will Crockett, isn't it?" Marshal Osborne said to Ward.

"Why do you think my brother would kill someone who was practically raised in our house?" Gid asked.

Crawford shook his head. "I'm sorry, Crockett, but the clues are overwhelming."

"What sort of clues?"

"Sheriff McMurtry was killed by one bullet. One bullet, and one bullet only had been fired from your brother's gun. The prisoner they were escorting was hanging from a nearby tree. Will Crockett reeked of whiskey, and the empty bottle was found near him."

"We know he was disappointed because O'Neal wasn't

sentenced to hang," Marshal Osborne added. "So what we figure happened, was that Crockett tried to talk the sheriff into hanging O'Neal, and when the sheriff wouldn't go along with it, your brother killed him, and hung O'Neal himself."

"Then he just stood there, waiting on you to come find him?" Gid asked.

"Well, that's where the whiskey comes in," Crawford said. "We figure Crockett got drunk to celebrate, then passed out, and came to just before we arrived. Of course, he wasn't expecting us to be there."

"He didn't do it," Gid insisted.

"Well, he's a wanted man now, whether he did it or not," Osborne said. "He resisted arrest. If he was innocent, he wouldn't have run away."

"He didn't do it," Gid repeated.

"Do you know where he is?" Osborne asked.

"No."

"If you know where he is, you are bound by law to tell us. Otherwise, you would be aiding and abetting, in which case you would share his guilt."

"I wouldn't tell you if I did know," Gid said.

"Do you two plan to stay in Tilden?" Ward asked Marshal Osborne. "What are you going to do?"

"The first thing we're going to do is send telegrams to the sheriffs of every adjacent county, then notify both the

U.S. Marshal's offices, as well as the Texas Rangers. We will ask them to pick up, and hold Will Crockett, until we can come for him. Sheriff McMurtry was a well-liked man, and once the news gets out that Crockett murdered the sheriff, I expect everyone will be on the lookout for him. Oh, and Deputy Haller?"

"Yes?"

"We will expect full cooperation from you."

Ward didn't reply, but just stood there watching as the two U.S. Marshals left.

"Those two sons of bitches wouldn't know a clue if it was sticking out of their ass," Gid said.

"I need to stop by and pick-up Anna so I can take her with me to see Lucy," Ward said. "Do you want to stay here for a while? I think your deputy's appointment is still valid. You could take care of any business that might come in."

Gid nodded his head.

* * *

Ward and Anna walked up to the house on the corner of Ash and Congress.

"Thanks for coming with me, Anna," Ward said. "I don't know if I could do this by myself."

"It has to be done," Anna said, reaching out to take

231

Ward's hand in hers.

Squaring his shoulders in preparation for the ordeal, Ward walked up onto the front porch and knocked on the door.

"Ward, Anna," Lucy said, greeting them with a smile. "How nice to see you. Is Ty with you?"

Ward and Anna exchanged glances and when Ward looked back toward Lucy, the expression on his face told it all. She put her hand over her heart, and her eyes filled with tears.

"No," she said. "Oh, please, God, not again."

For just a second Ward was confused by what she meant by "again", then he remembered that her husband, a Texas Ranger, had been killed in the line of duty.

Lucy put her arms around Ward and though, for just a moment he was unsure of what he should do, he put his arms around her too, and let her cry on his shoulder.

"Lucy, I'm so sorry," Anna said, as her own eyes filled with tears.

Lucy moved from Ward to Anna, now weeping with all the pain of a broken heart.

"Where is he?" Lucy asked. "I want to see him."

"He's with Lonnie right now."

"Please, take me to see him."

"Oh, Lucy, wouldn't you rather wait until he's ready to be viewed?" Anna asked.

"Take me to him now, please," Lucy repeated.

"All right," Ward agreed. "I'll take you."

As Ward and Lucy walked toward the undertaking establishment, Lucy reached out to take his hand. He let her squeeze his hand as hard as she wanted to.

When they reached Welsh's, he turned to her.

"Wait here for just a moment while I speak to Lonnie."

"Ward, please, say whatever needs to be said. I want to see him. I must see him."

"All right, you have a seat there, I'll talk to him."

When Ward stepped into the embalming room, he saw Ty lying on the table. His shirt was removed where Lonnie had washed away blood from the wound.

"Ward, what do you need?" Lonnie asked.

"Lonnie, Lucy McPheters is here. She wants to see Ty."

"Can't she just wait for the viewing, like everyone else?"

"She wants some time alone with him."

"Why would she . . . oh, yes, I understand. Tell her to give me just a moment."

"Can I see him?" Lucy asked when Ward returned to the reception room.

"Yes, in just a minute."

Lucy began wringing the handkerchief in her hands as she waited. Less than a minute later, Lonnie came into the room. "Mrs. McPheters, you can come with me."

233

"Thank you."

Lonnie started back with her.

"No, please, give me a moment alone with him."

"Well, that's not the way it's usually done, at least, not before he's ready for viewing."

"Please, Mr. Welsh, I beg of you."

Lonnie looked at her for a moment, then he made a single nod of his head. "All right, he's in the room on the right."

"Thank you."

Lucy stepped into the embalming room which, because there were no windows, had two lanterns for light. Ty was lying on the table, his skin glowing gold in the diffused light. There was a sheet draped over him from his shoulders down and she started to remove it, but decided to leave it in place.

"Oh, Ty, my precious sweetheart," she said, her voice breaking. "I've had two loves, and both have been taken from me by murder. You will see Norman in heaven; tell him that I had enough love in my heart for both of you. He was a good man, and he will understand."

Will returned to the scene where he and Ty had been ambushed. Ty's body had been moved, but he was surprised to see that O'Neal was still hanging from the tree.

"Why'd they do it, O'Neal? Why did they take you

from us just to hang you? And why did they kill Ty, and leave me alive?

"And how did Baker wind up with them?" he added, still musing aloud.

He began wandering around, looking for any clue that might lead him back to Felton and the others, but he found nothing helpful. He looked back at O'Neal's body, wondering if he should cut it down, then decided against it, thinking at least as long as the body was hanging there, none of the scavenging animals would be able to get to it.

Any further musing was interrupted when he heard a wagon approaching. Getting out of sight, he watched to see who it was, and what they wanted.

There were two men with the wagon. Will recognized Dan Evans as the driver, but he had never seen the other man.

"There he is," Dan said.

"How are we going to get him down from there?"

"One of is going to have to shinny up the tree and cut him down," Dan said.

"One of us?"

"You're the youngest."

"Yeah, I thought you would say that."

Dan chuckled. "Why do you think I brought you, Paul? It sure as hell wasn't just to have somebody to talk to."

The one called Paul climbed the tree, then out on the

branch far enough to allow him to cut down the body.

"They're sayin' Will Crockett hung this fella."

"I know what they're sayin'."

"Do you think he did it?"

"I don't know, but I sure doubt it," Dan replied. "They're a saying that Crockett was some upset that the judge didn't sentence O'Neal to hang, 'n they're sayin' he took it on hisself to do it, 'n when the sheriff tried to stop him, why he shot 'im. But I met Will Crockett 'n I took the measure of the man. I don't believe he did what they're sayin'. There ain't no way Will Crockett done this."

"They've written books about the Crocketts, did you know that?"

"No, I never heard that," Dan said.

"Yep, they sure have. Ned Buntline wrote 'em. I've read some of 'em. Will 'n Gid Crockett are heroes in them books. It's kind of hard for me to believe that somebody Ned Buntline wrote about as a hero would do somethin' like this."

"And I'm tellin' you, Will Crockett never done this."

"How do you know he didn't do it?"

"I just know it."

"All I can say is this. I never met Will Crockett, but I did know Ty McMurtry, 'n he was one of the best men I ever know'd. So if this feller Will Crockett did kill 'im, then I think he should be hung, just like this feller that he hung."

"He didn't do it," Dan said.

Will wanted to thank Dan, and he would have if Dan had been alone. So he remained hidden, and watched as they loaded O'Neal's body in the wagon, and headed for Tilden.

Ward, who was now the temporary sheriff, was sitting at the sheriff's desk. Gid, who had remained in the office while Ward had informed Lucy of Ty's death, was still there.

"If five men were standing right here in front of us, swearing on a stack of Bibles that they had actually seen Will shoot Ty, I wouldn't believe them," Gid said.

"I don't think I would believe them either," Ward said. "Ty spoke so highly of you and Will, and how well he remembered the childhood he shared with you two."

"I was in love with his sister," Gid said.

"You say you *were* in love with her. What happened?"

"The war happened," Gid said.

"I was too young for the war," Ward said. "And I was too young to realize how fortunate I was to have missed it."

The front door opened, and Coy Prosser came into the office.

"Haller," Coy said in loud and demanding voice. "I need you to turn over a couple o' them scatter guns you got there, 'n a couple boxes of shells. Double aught buckshot, not the bird shot I got peppered with."

"Now just why in the Sam Hill would I want to do something like that?" Ward asked.

"Cause I'm headin' up a posse to go after that murderin' son of a bitch, 'n if he gives us any trouble when we find him, I'll blow his ass away with a twelve gauge Greener."

"You'll not be getting any shotguns, and I've given no authorization to form a posse to go after Will Crockett," Ward said, resolutely.

"'Didn't need no authorization from you," Coy said. "I been authorized by Marshal Crawford, 'n I reckon his authority is a little bit higher 'n yours is."

"All right, go with your posse, but you'll be getting no shotguns from me."

"Yeah, well, we don't really need no shotguns," Coy said. "A rifle or a pistol will kill the son of a bitch just as dead."

"Prosser, if you harm my brother, you'll deal with me," Gid said in defiance.

"Ha! I ain't worried none 'bout no cripple comin' after me," Coy taunted.

Chapter Twenty-five

It was late in the evening, and Gid was in The Tinder-box Saloon. There were fewer than usual people in the saloon right now because several had joined the posse Coy Prosser had formed. It was no coincidence that many of the posse were the same people who had been a part of the lynch mob that Will had stopped from taking out Paddy O'Neal.

Gid was sitting at a table with Millie Jean and Sara Sue Sanders, nursing the only beer he had bought.

"If it's any consolation to you, Gid, I don't think he did it," Millie Jean said.

"I don't either," Sara Sue added.

"I know damn well he didn't do it," Gid said. "Oh, excuse the language, ladies," he added.

Both Millie Jean and Sara Sue laughed. Millie Jean put her hand on Gid's. "Honey, you don't have to ask to be excused for anything. You and your brother are two of the nicest men we've ever met. You treat us as if we actually are ladies instead of," she paused before she said the next word, "whores."

Gid thought of Katie, and what might have been. He covered her hand with his other hand. "You are ladies," he said with quiet intensity.

There was a stable behind the doctor's office, in which Dr. Burke kept the horse he used to draw his buggy. Will, who had sneaked into town in the night, put his horse there, then, after making certain he wasn't seen, stepped inside the office and went back to the room Gid had been occupying.

"He isn't here," a woman's voice said, and turning, Will saw Anna.

"Where is he?"

"I believe he is down at The Tinderbox."

"I don't expect it would be a good idea for me to go down there right now."

Anna grinned. "No, I don't think it would."

"Anna, I didn't . . ." Will was stopped in mid-sentence by Anna's raised hand.

"Oh, for heaven's sake, Will, you don't have to tell me you didn't kill the sheriff. I've seen the two of you together—I know what great friends you were."

"Thank you," Will said. "Well, if Gid isn't here, I guess I'll just . . ."

"Go down to the cellar," Anna said.

"What?"

"You have to be somewhere. You can wait on Gid there."

"Thanks."

"Will?"

It wasn't until Gid spoke to him that Will realized he had been asleep.

"Wow," Gid said with a little chuckle. "You were sleeping hard."

"I didn't get much sleep last night."

"I can imagine. What happened, Will?"

Will told about being ambushed by Felton and his gang, and of his shock when he saw them hang O'Neal, one of their own.

"Who killed Ty?"

"As far as who actually pulled the trigger, I don't know, because I was knocked out. Ty was dead, when I came to."

"I figured it had to be something like that."

"Gid, Martin Baker was with them."

"What?" Gid asked in surprise. "How in the world did he wind up way over here? And why?"

"For now, the how and why is a mystery. But he is here."

241

"Will, are you hungry?" Anna asked, coming down the stairs.

"As a matter of fact, I am."

Anna smiled. "I thought you might be. I brought some fried chicken and biscuits for you."

"Uh, did you bring…" Gid started, but Anna answered his question before he finished asking.

"Yes, I brought enough for both of you."

"Thank you, Anna," Will said.

"I'll bring you breakfast in the morning."

Because it would attract unwanted attention if all five men rode into Beeville as a group, Felton broke them up so that they didn't all ride into town together. Paxton and Jamie Kildeer came in from the north, while Scarborough and Baker came in from the south. Felton came in alone.

Felton went into the bank first, then walked up to the table as if writing a check. Scarborough and Baker came in next, then Paxton. Jamie Kildeer was still out front, now holding the reins to the other four horses.

When the other three men were in the bank, Felton gave a nod, and all four men drew their pistols.

"This is a holdup!" Felton shouted.

"Oh!" one of the two tellers cried out.

Paxton and Baker approached the two tellers carrying cloth bags. "Fill 'em up," Felton ordered.

With shaking hands, the tellers emptied their cash drawers.

"Now the safe," Felton said walking up to one of the tellers.

"I can't," the teller answered.

Felton shot him.

"The safe," he said to the other teller. The other teller hurried over to the safe, opened it, then took out all the money and dropped it in the cloth bags.

"For that, I'll let you live," Felton said.

With money bags in hand, the four men hurried out of the bank, then got mounted.

"How much did we get?" Jamie asked with a broad grin.

"It won't matter to you," Felton said, as he shot Jamie.

As they galloped away, the four robbers hurrahed the town by shooting at pedestrians, and into buildings. They got away cleanly.

"Who were they?" Sheriff Briggs asked Jamie.

Jamie was lying in the street in front of the bank, bleeding from a chest wound. He didn't answer Sheriff Brigg's question.

"Son, they're the ones that shot you. Are you going to let them get away with it?"

"No, I'm not," Jamie said. "It was Jess Felton, a man called Paxton, Ben Scarborough, and Martin Baker."

Jamie coughed, and blood came from his mouth. "'N here's somethin' else Felton done. Look in my pocket, you'll find somethin' I took from the sheriff. That ought to prove that I was there so's you can believe me when I tell you. Felton is the one that hung O'Neal 'n he's the one that killt Sheriff McMurtry. It warn't Will Crockett."

There was another spasm of coughing, more blood, then Jamie Kildeer took his last breath.

By now there were at least half a dozen others from the town who had gathered around the body in the street.

"Did you men hear what he said about who killed Sheriff McMurtry?" Sheriff Briggs asked.

All nodded in the affirmative.

"Remember it, you may need to make a statement."

Will had spent three days in the cellar, but he knew he couldn't stay much longer. For one thing he was beginning to feel too closed in, and for another thing, he didn't want to get Gid and Anna in trouble for hiding him. Dr. Burke would be safe, because he didn't even know that Will was here.

Along with the food, Anna had also brought him a few books to read, and at the moment he was reading, *Dr. Breen's Practice*, a novel by William Dean Howells.

"Hello, Will."

Will looked up to see Deputy Ward Haller.

"Deputy," Will said, calmly.

"Actually, he's the sheriff now," a grinning Gid said, coming down the stairs behind Haller.

"What is it?" Will asked. "What's going on?"

"I thought you might like to see this telegram," Ward said, holding out a yellow piece of paper.

BEEVILLE BANK ROBBED BY FELTON GANG TELLER KILLED CONFESSION OF JAMIE KILDEER MEMBER OF FELTON GANG SAYS FELTON KILLED O'NEAL AND SHERIFF McMURTRY

SHERIFF BRIGGS, BEESVILE

"Jamie Kildeer, huh?" Will said as he examined the telegram. "It's hard to believe that he would clear me. He told me he was Ed Kildeer's brother, and he blamed me for killing him."

"It was a matter of priorities, I suppose," Ward said. "You killed his brother, but Felton killed him."

"Yeah, I guess that makes sense." Then, looking at Gid, he just noticed something. "Gid, you're walking without a crutch."

"Let's go get a beer. I'll show you how well I can walk."

Will, Gid, and Ward walked down to The Tinderbox.

"Wait out here for a second," Ward said. "You'd better let me go in first."

As soon as Ward went into the saloon he held both hands up. "Folks, let me have your attention for a moment," he called out.

All conversation halted as everyone looked over toward the new sheriff.

"I'm about to bring Will Crockett in, and I don't want any of you to get too excited. Will has been cleared. We now know that Sheriff McMurtry was killed by Jess Felton." Ward turned toward the batwing doors. "You two come on in."

As soon as Will and Gid stepped into the saloon, the others in the saloon cheered.

"Will!" Millie Jean called as she and Sara Sue ran toward him, a big smile on their faces, and with their arms outstretched. Both women gave him a welcoming hug.

"Come over here, Will," Clyde called out to him. "Your beer is on the house."

"I've got a better idea," Will said. "Drinks for everyone in the house are on me."

Again, the saloon patrons cheered as they hurried toward the bar.

"And that includes the young ladies," Will added. "In fact, there are twelve people in here. They don't have to drink them, but I'll be buying twelve drinks for each of the ladies."

"I'm glad you said that we didn't have to drink all of

them," Millie Jean said. "I just don't think I could drink that much tea."

"Tea?" one of the saloon patrons said. "You mean when I buy you a drink, it ain't nothin' but tea?"

"Heavens, honey, if we actually drank whiskey all day, we'd be so drunk we couldn't even walk. Besides, what difference does it make to you what we drink? It's our company you're paying for."

Several of the other patrons laughed. "Looks to me like she got you there, Carl," one of the others said.

"You three come sit with us," Millie Jean invited.

"I can't, I'd better get back to the office," Ward said.

"That's all right, they were just being nice. They didn't want to sit with you anyway, they just wanted to sit with Will 'n me," Gid said with a little chuckle.

"And I'm not sure the doctor's daughter wouldn't want that anyway," Sara Sue added.

Shortly after the four of them took a seat, Doodle came over to the table.

"Doodle, you aren't going to cause any trouble, are you?" Millie Jean asked.

Doodle shook his head, and held up his hands, one of them holding a beer.

"No, I just wanted to thank this one for the beer," Doodle said, looking at Will, then with a broad grin on his face, he nodded toward Gid. "Besides, there ain't no way in hell I'm goin' to ever tangle with this big son of a bitch again." His laughter as he spoke, removed any animus from the appellation.

The next afternoon, Will and Gid were visiting with Ward in the sheriff's office, when the door opened and someone came in.

"Sheriff Briggs," Ward said. "This is a surprise, seeing you in our neck of the woods. Will, you can thank this gentleman for clearing your name."

"And these two must be the famous Crockett brothers," the sheriff said.

"That's right—Will and Gid. Will is the little one."

Sheriff Briggs laughed. "Little one? If you introduced him to me anywhere else, he would more than likely be the big one. But alongside this fella, I guess I can see your point."

"What brings you to Tilden?"

"I was hoping you'd help me bring in the Felton gang. They killed one of our bank tellers when they robbed the bank the other day and they killed that kid they had ridin' with 'em," the sheriff said. "Claude Potter was a good man, and I wouldn't want to see them get away with that."

"They killed a couple of good men from here, too," Ward said. "As it happens, Ty had brought Will and Gid in to help him go after Felton, and the three of us were just now discussing what to do next."

"By the way, have you ever seen this before?"

Sheriff Briggs showed Ward a small pen knife.

"Sure, I've seen that. I gave Ty that little knife for his last birthday."

"Good, that should be all that's needed if any question ever comes up about Mr. Crockett."

"What do you mean?"

"The boy, Jamie Kildeer, said that he took this from Sheriff McMurtry's pocket. This knife puts him on the scene when the sheriff was killed, so we can believe the statement he made just before he died was the truth. He said Felton was the one who hanged O'Neal and then he used Will's gun to kill Sheriff McMurtry."

Will smiled broadly. "Sheriff Briggs, I don't care what anyone else might say about you, I think you're a damn good man."

Chapter Twenty-six

In the cabin that Felton was using for a hideout, he finished counting the money. "Four thousand dollars," Felton said. "That breaks down to eight-hundred dollars apiece, counting Jamie Kildeer's share. But seeing as he ain't here, I'll take his share too."

"Kildeer ain't here, on account of 'cause you killt 'im," Scarborough said.

Felton smiled. "Exactly. So who better to get his share?"

"What did you shoot 'im for?" Baker asked.

"You got a problem with that?"

Baker remembered how he was shot by Clem Cassidy and then left for dead. He didn't think it was right for him to get shot, and he didn't think it was right for the boy to get shot. But he kept any censure of the action to himself.

"That don't seem right to me that you get his whole share," Scarborough said.

"You can leave, if you want to," Felton said. "And the rest of us will divide up your share."

"No, no, it's all good," Scarborough said quickly, holding his hands out to show that he had abandoned any complaint he may have had.

"This is all good too," Paxton said as he stuffed his money into his pocket, "but . . ."

"But you want more," Felton said.

"Yeah. I mean I was kind of hopin' to make a big score here, then goin' up to Wyoming, or out to California or some such place 'n maybe buyin' me a small ranch."

"Ranch hell," Baker said. "That's work, even iffen you own the ranch. I plan to buy me a saloon."

"Yeah, well, eight hunnert dollars ain't enough to buy no ranch or a saloon," Paxton said.

"I've got another job comin' up," Felton said.

"When?" Paxton asked.

"Soon."

"What's the job?"

"I'll tell you when you need to know."

* * *

That same evening Coy Prosser and the six men who had joined his posse were sitting around a campfire, eating the two rabbits they had killed.

"If you ask me, we're just a' wastin' our time," Amon Parker said, as he ripped some of the meat off the bone he was holding.

"Why do you say that?" Prosser challenged.

"On account of they's no way Will Crockett would still be hangin' aroun' here. He's more 'n likely two, maybe three counties away from here by now. Hell, he's prob'ly done gone up into the Indian Territory, or maybe Arkansas or some such."

"Nah, there ain't no way he's left," Prosser insisted.

"How do you know?"

"On account of his brother is still healin' up in the doc's office, 'n you ain't never seen no brothers closer 'n them two is. Will Crockett ain't plannin' on leavin' him."

"Yeah, I think you're right," one of the others said.

"You know what? If we ain't found 'im in a couple of days, we ought to maybe go back into town 'n see if Haller's heard anything about 'im," Parker said.

"Better yet, seein' as how close them two brothers is, why don't we go get a' holt of Will Crocket's brother 'n hold on to 'im. Will Crockett's bound to find out, 'n when he comes in to check on 'im, we'll be a' waitin' for 'im," Arnie Purcell said.

"Huh, uh," Jaco said, shaking his head. "I ain't messin' with that big son of a bitch again."

"What if we do find 'im? I mean, what if we find 'im

'n take 'im back, 'n somehow he's able to talk his way out of it?"

Prosser laughed. "Hell, Higgins, I thought you knowed what was goin' to happen."

"You thought I knowed what?"

"When we take his ass back, he won't be sayin' nothin' at all, on account of the son of a bitch will be dead, 'n dead men don't talk."

The night creatures called to each other as Felton and the others sat astride their horses just outside Oakville. A cloud passed over the moon, then moved away, bathing in silver the little town that rose up like a ghost before them. The largest building in town, larger even than the hotel, was a big white house that stood at the end of the street with its cupolas, dormers, balconies, porches, and gingerbread trim, all shining brightly in the moonlight. The property was surrounded by a white picket fence which enclosed, not only the house, but a carriage house and stable as well.

"Let's go," Felton said. "We'll tie the horses off in the stable at the back of the property. That way no one will notice any strange horses hangin' around the house."

The four men rode slowly into town, avoiding the main street and approaching from an angle that would be least likely to be noticed. When they reached the stable behind the big, white house, they dismounted, and then took care of the horses. One of the stabled horses snorted, as if questioning these uninvited guests, but the interrogation died with one whicker.

"Paxton, you and Scarborough stay outside here, and keep an eye out. Baker and I will go into the house and take care of business," Felton said.

From the shadows of the stable the four men moved out into the bright moonlight, picking their way carefully and quietly across the back yard. Paxton and Scarborough went toward the front then stayed just behind the corner on each side of the house where they could see the street, but no one on the street would be able to see them. As soon as the two men were in position, Felton and Baker stepped up onto the back porch. The back door to the house was locked, but Felton stuck his knife in between the door edge and the lock plate and had it open in a couple of seconds.

They slipped inside. This was the kitchen, and the big cookstove loomed over one side of the room, giving off a faint aroma of the pork that had recently been cooked. There was a white cloth at one end of the table, and as they walked by, Baker lifted the cloth. Under the cloth was a plate with a couple of cold pork chops and half a pan of biscuits.

Baker grabbed a pork chop, pulled the meat away from

the bone, then stuck it into a biscuit. He dropped the bone where he stood. Eating his impromptu supper, he followed Felton through the rest of the house.

A spill of moonlight illuminated the parlor and showed, clearly, the bottom of the stairs. They started up the stairs and were on the third step when there was a sudden whirring sound, followed by two "bongs." It was the clock, striking two A.M.

"Son-of-a-bitch," Baker whispered. "That scared the hell out of me."

"Keep quiet," Felton warned.

They continued to the top of the stairs. Slowly, quietly, they moved to the nearest bedroom, then opened the door. The same splash of moonlight that had illuminated the parlor, also illuminated this room and they could see a woman, sleeping alone.

"What the hell? Where's Coleman?" Baker asked, surprised to see the woman alone.

Baker started on down the hall.

"Where you goin'?" Felton asked.

"To look for Coleman," Baker answered.

"No need for that. The woman's all we need."

Quietly, Felton and Baker moved on into the room, then stood over the bed, looking down at her.

The woman woke with a start and looking up to see Felton staring down at her, tried to scream, only to have it cut off by increased pressure from Felton's hand.

"You just lay there real quiet-like and you won't get hurt," Felton hissed in the darkness.

The woman's eyes were opened wide in terror.

"Where at's your husband?"

She continued to stare at him with fear-crazed eyes.

"He in the house?"

The woman made no attempt to answer, and Felton cocked his pistol.

"Shake your head yes or no, lady," Felton said gruffly. "Is he in the house?"

The woman shook her head yes.

"I'm goin' to take my hand away now," Felton said. "If you so much as make a peep, I'm goin' to blow your brains out. Then I'm goin' to kill your husband and then your kid. You got that?" Slowly, he pulled his hand away.

"What . . . what do you want?" the woman asked in a small, frightened voice.

"I want you to take me into your husband's room. Then I want you to wake him up."

The woman nodded, then got out of bed.

Felton and Baker followed her out of her room, across the hall, and into the bedroom of her husband, where they heard loud snoring.

"Wake him up."

"Edward? Edward?" the woman said in a soft voice.

The snoring halted for a moment, then continued.

"I said wake him up, lady."

"Edward!" She placed her hand on his arm as she spoke.

Coleman snorted and wheezed. "What?" he asked. "What is it?"

"There are some men here."

"What?" He moved his head where he could see his wife.

"I said there are some men here in the house," the woman said, her voice breaking with fear.

"What do you mean, men?" Edward reached for the bedside lantern, lit it, then turned it up so that the room was bathed in light. Then he picked up his glasses and put them on, fitting them very carefully over one ear at a time. That was when he saw the two men standing by his wife. "My God!" he gasped, jumping up quickly. "What are you doing in my bedroom? In my house?"

"This here's a bank robbery, Mr. Coleman," Felton said easily.

"What do you mean a bank robbery? Are you crazy? I don't keep any money here."

"I know you don't. But you own the bank don't ya? And this here's your wife ain't she?" Felton pointed the gun toward the woman's head, putting the barrel against her temple. "Now what I want you to do is, go down there to your bank, get all the money out of your safe, then bring it back right here. I'll be sending one of my men with you to make certain you get it all. Do you understand?"

"Why on earth would I want to do a damn fool thing like that?"

"Because if you don't bring the money back, I'm gonna kill your wife and your kid right here in front of you," Felton growled. "And then I aim to kill you, too."

"I'm . . . I'm not at all sure I can even do what you are asking," Edward Coleman stammered. "The money is in a vault, and it has a difficult lock. I don't normally open it, because I leave that to my chief teller."

"You'd damn well better figure it out," Felton said easily, "'cause if you ain't back in half-an-hour, we kill the woman and then the kid."

"Edward, for heavens' sake, do what they ask," the woman said, her voice breaking with fear.

"Just be calm, Martha," Coleman said. "I don't believe they really mean you any harm."

"That depends. If you ain't back with the money before that clock strikes three, we're goin' to kill her."

"All right, all right," Coleman said, holding his hands out toward them. "Let me get dressed and then I'll go."

Quickly, Coleman pulled on his trousers and a shirt, then he slipped on his shoes. Finally, he was ready to go.

"Remember, before the clock strikes three, or the woman dies. Baker, go down and tell Paxton to go with him."

"You want me to go too, Felton?"

"No, I want you to come back here and find the kid."

After Coleman left, Felton looked over at Martha. Her eyes reflected her terror, but she was fighting hard to keep herself under control.

"You're keeping quiet. That's real good," Felton said.

"I don't want to awaken the baby," Martha said.

"Awaken," Felton said with a malevolent smile. "Is that rich folks talk for wakin' somebody up?"

Martha didn't answer.

Baker came back into the room. "Paxton 'n him is on the way," Baker said.

"Baker, tie her hands behind the chair."

"That won't be necessary," Martha said. "I won't give you any trouble."

"You damn right you won't," Felton said. He tossed a short piece of rope to Baker. "Do what I said."

Baker pulled Martha's arms around behind the chair, then tied her hands.

"Tell you what, let's gag 'er, too," Felton said.

"What'll I use as a gag?"

Felton pointed to Coleman's pajama's lying on his bed. "Use the top of his pajamas."

Bound and gagged, Martha watched with wide-open, terrified eyes as the two men paced back and forth in the room, occasionally stepping over to the window to look outside.

After about the tenth time, Baker walked over to look out the window.

"There they are," he said. "They're comin' back."

"Is he carrying anything?" Felton asked.

"Paxton's carryin' a big sack."

Felton smiled, broadly. "That's our money! Son of a bitch, Baker! We done it! We took this bank!"

Paxton and Coleman came into the house, then up the stairs.

"I emptied the safe," Coleman said.

"He's tellin' the truth, Jess," Paxton said. "I looked into the safe 'n there warn't nothin' left. I don't know how much it was, 'cause I didn't have time to count it. I just know it's a lot."

"We can count it when we get back to the cabin," Felton said.

"Can we stop and spend some of it in Los Lomas? There don't nobody know us there," Paxton said.

"That's too close to the cabin, ain't it?" Baker asked.

Coleman looked at his wife. "You can let her go now," he said. He reached for the gag.

"No, leave it there. I don't want her screamin' when we kill you."

"What? But wait, I did as you . . . uhnn!"

Coleman's gasp came as Baker stabbed him.

Martha tried to scream, but she could do little more than squeak around her gag.

"I think it's best that we leave you tied up and gagged," Felton said. "'Cause if we take it off, 'n you start in a' screamin' we'll have to kill you, too. And then who's gonna take care of your kid? A fine house like this, someone'll come nosin' around soon enough."

"You know," Paxton said. "She's a fine-lookin' woman, maybe we should have a little fun with her."

"Paxton, you ain't got good sense," Felton said. "We got what we came for, so let's get out of here."

Chapter Twenty-seven

Martha sat still for a long time, not sure but what they may have left one of their men behind to take care of her if she caused any trouble.

She saw her husband lying on the floor, his back covered with blood.

Oh Edward, what am I going to do without you? How am I going to raise our baby without you?

Martha cried, quietly, until she was all cried out. Then, she began working on the ropes and was able to free herself just as the room began to grow light. That was also when her baby began crying.

Martha got dressed, then with the baby in her arms, walked down to the sheriff's office.

Sheriff Algood was having breakfast at his desk when Martha walked in.

"Miz Coleman, what brings you out so early in the.. .?"

When Sheriff Algood saw the expression on Martha's face, he stopped in mid-question. "Martha, what is it? What's wrong?" the sheriff asked, dropping all formality.

"They killed him, Matt," Martha said. "They killed Edward."

It had been three days since Sheriff Briggs had come to Tilden to offer the evidence that cleared Will once and for all. Now, Will and Gid were in Beeville, dismounting in front of the sheriff's office.

"Do you think the sheriff will have any information that we can use?" Gid asked.

"Well, as far as I'm concerned, he's already provided the most important information," Will said. "He proved my innocence."

"That's true," Gid said.

"So, whether he has anything else that can help us or not, I think that I owe him dinner."

"Yeah," Gid said. "I like that idea."

Will laughed. "I thought you would, Little Brother."

Sheriff Briggs was leaning back in his chair with his feet resting on his desk when Will and Gid opened the door. The sheriff reacted quickly as if he was ashamed to have one of the citizens of the town find him in such an unprofessional position. Then, when he recognized his visitors, the look of embarrassment on his face changed to a smile.

"Will, Gid," he said, getting up from his desk and walking over to greet the two men with an extended hand. "What brings you two to Beeville?"

"We're back in the hunt for Jess Felton and his gang," Will said.

"Yeah? Well, I sure as hell hope you catch them. The teller they killed here was Claude Potter. He had two kids, one of 'em still a babe in arms. It's been just real hard on his widow. Fact is, I hear she's so upset she can't even nurse, now, so she's got another woman wet nursin' for her."

"We'd like to pick your brain a little," Will said. "I thought we might buy your dinner if you've got the time."

Briggs smiled. "Why, that would be just real nice of you to do that. I know where we should go."

As Will, Gid, and Sheriff Briggs were making plans to go to eat, Coy Prosser, Amon Parker, Harry Walls, Jaco Miller, and Arnie Stone were riding into Tilden. They were just returning after having spent two weeks in a fruitless search for Will Crockett.

"I'm so thirsty that I'm going to drink so much beer that Clyde will have to tap into another keg," Jaco said, as the men tied off their horses in front of The Tinderbox Saloon.

The six men were greeted by the saloon's patrons when they walked in.

"Prosser, damn, where the hell have all you boys been?" someone called out to them.

"Hell, you know where we've been, Benton. We've been lookin' for that son of a bitch Will Crockett," Prosser said. "And when we catch that bastard, believe me, he will pay for murderin' Sheriff McMurtry."

"Wait a minute," Clyde said. "You mean you haven't heard? Hell, I thought that was why you wasn't a comin' in."

"Heard what?" Prosser asked.

"I guess it makes sense why you men haven't heard, what with you boys havin' been gone for what, nigh on to two weeks now? Anyhow, as it turns out, Will Crockett didn't do it. He's been cleared."

"What the hell do you mean, he's been cleared? Who cleared him?"

"The Bank of Beeville was held up last week, 'n one of the bank robbers was shot. Just before he died, he said it was Felton that killed the sheriff."

"Wait a minute, are you sayin' that one of Felton's outlaws is sayin' that it was Felton hisself, what killt the sheriff? And he also hung O'Neal, I suppose."

"Yes, that too. That's what the man said."

"And folks is a' believin' that?"

"Why not? He was there, and he saw it," Clyde said. "Unlike those two marshals who didn't see it."

"What do you mean they didn't see it? Them two marshals caught Will Crockett red-handed at the scene of the crime," Prosser said. "The sheriff was dead, and O'Neal was already hung."

"No, they found him there *after* the crime was already committed, so they didn't actual see anythin'," one of the other patrons said. "But the feller that told Sheriff Briggs about it, well now, it turns out he actual seen Felton kill the sheriff. Anyway, I never thought Crockett done it in the first place. I don't think he has it in him to do somethin' like that, especially to one of his best friends."

"You're talkin' about the same son of a bitch that filled my chest with a load of buckshot," Prosser said.

"It warn't buckshot, Prosser, it was birdshot," one of the men said. "Iffen it had been buckshot you'd be dead now. Besides which, he done that to keep you from hangin' O'Neal. 'N when you stop to think about it, it don't hardly make no sense that he'd stop you from hangin' O'Neal, then turn right around 'n do it his ownself, does it?"

"Come on, Coy, let's get us a beer, then go sit down 'n look at the pretty girls," Purcell invited.

Prosser stood there for a moment longer, the expression on his face reflecting his anger.

"You comin' or not?" Purcell asked.

"Yeah, I'm comin'," Prosser said. He pointed to Clyde. "But there ain't no way I'm believin' that Will Crockett ain't the bastard that killt McMurtry. 'N I ain't givin' up huntin' for the son of a bitch neither."

Jaco had been listening to, but not taking part in the conversation, when he heard someone calling to him.

"Jaco, over here," Doodle called, holding up his hand in invitation.

Jaco took his beer and left the others to join his friend at his table.

"So, how was the big hunt for Crockett?" Doodle asked.

"You ought to be glad you weren't with us," Jaco said as he sat down. "Skeeters, fire ants, rain, nothin' to eat but beans from a can, yes sir, you was the smart one, all right."

"Plus even if you found 'im, when you brought 'im back you'd 'a had to let 'im go, because of the fact that he didn't even do it," Doodle said.

"Yeah, that's what Clyde was a' sayin'. On account of that, I guess it's just a real good thing we didn' find 'im, on account of Prosser was plannin' on killin' 'im a'fore we even had a chance to bring 'im back."

"Damn, Jaco, you warn't goin' to do nothin' like that, was you? I mean kill 'im, even a'fore he went to trial?"

"Well, he's wanted dead or alive, so it wouldn't a' got us in trouble or nothin' if we did kill 'im. 'N from all I've heard about 'im, that would a' been the safest way to bring 'im back."

Back in Beeville, Will and Gid were walking down to the Busy Bee, to fulfill their offer of supper for Sheriff Briggs. Sheriff Briggs was quite a popular man in Beeville, as evidenced by all the greetings he received before, and even after the three of them stepped into the café.

"You folks sure seem to have a thing about bees," Gid said. "Bee County, Beeville, and the Busy Bee Restaurant."

"It could be worse," Sheriff Briggs said. "It could be the Cockroach Restaurant."

"Ha, you didn't think of that now did you Little Brother."

They were shown to an empty table by a matron-ly-looking woman whom Sheriff Briggs addressed as Wilma.

"I believe you said you wanted to pick my brain, so go ahead, you're welcome to what little of it there is," Sheriff Briggs said with a self-deprecating laugh as they took their seats around the table.

"Yes, we're trying to gather as much information on Jess Felton as we can."

"Isn't everyone? I don't know as I can give you much

more information than is generally known," Briggs said.

"To begin with, how do you know that it was Felton, and not someone else?" Will asked.

"That one's easy. When he hit our bank, some of the citizens of the town recognized him. Actually, three of the riders were recognized, but nobody was able to identify the fourth."

"Who are the ones they recognized?"

"Felton, of course. Also Paxton and Scarborough."

"Paxton and Scarborough? What do they look like?"

"Paxton's an ordinary size feller, 'n he's got kind 'a squinty eyes, 'n a pointy chin."

Will nodded his head. "That description fits one of the men who attempted to hold up the stage, and he was also one of the men who lynched O'Neal."

"And one of the other fellers, Scarborough, is a big man, at least six feet four inches tall, and well over two hundred pounds. 'N that ain't fat weight neither. 'Peers to be all muscle. They say he got his nose cut off in a knife fight so's the only thing left is just sort of a flat, red blob with two holes. Someone said he had a snout that looks like a pig, 'n now that I think about it, that's prob'ly a purty good description."

"Yes, it's the Felton gang all right. The man you just described was definitely with them."

"And the fourth man—nobody seems to know anything about him," Sheriff Briggs continued.

"That would be Martin Baker," Will said. "I was surprised to see him with Felton when they stopped Ty and me on the road to Cotulla."

"Martin Baker?" Briggs shook his head. "Who's he? I don't think I know about him."

"We ran across him out in Toyah," Will said. "He escaped from jail and killed a deputy, so I expect he's on the run."

As they were eating their supper a boy, wearing a Western Union cap, came into the restaurant. After looking around for a moment, he saw the sheriff, then came over to his table.

"You have a telegram, Sheriff," the boy said.

Sheriff Briggs thanked the boy, gave him a nickel, and took the telegram.

"I'll be damn," he said after reading it.

"What is it?" Will asked.

"It's from Sheriff Algood. Felton and his men just robbed a bank up in Oakville."

"Where's that?"

"It's over in Live Oak County."

"And the sheriff is sure it was Felton?"

"Yeah, he left his mark."

"His mark?"

"He killed the banker."

Chapter Twenty-eight

Ward Haller had just poured himself a cup of coffee when Jaco Miller and Doodle Higgens came into the office.

"Hello, Miller, Higgens," Ward said by way of greeting. "What's up?"

"Where are the Crocketts?" Jaco asked.

Ward narrowed his eyes. "Aren't you part of the posse Prosser put together? Why do you need to know?" he asked, suspiciously.

"Folks is sayin' that Crockett didn't do it," Jaco said.

"That's true, Will Crockett has been cleared," Ward said.

"On account of that, I ain't a part of the posse no more."

Ward chuckled. "Yes, I guess that would be the case, seeing as the posse is no longer in existence."

"That ain't true," Jaco said.

"Are you doubting that Will has been cleared?" Ward

challenged.

"No, what I'm sayin' is, it ain't true when you said there weren't no more posse. Prosser—why he plans on keepin' it goin'. 'N here's the thing of it, Deputy. Prosser say's he ain't a' plannin' on bringin' Crockett back in alive."

"Where's Prosser now?"

"When me 'n Doodle left, he 'n the others was still down at The Tinderbox."

Ward stepped over to take his hat down from the peg. "Let's go have a talk with Mr. Prosser," he said as he put the hat on.

"Uh, no, I, uh, don't want to go with you. I don't think it would be good for Prosser 'n them others, to see me with you."

Ward nodded. "All right, I suppose I can see that."

Several Tilden citizens exchanged friendly greetings with Ward as he walked toward The Tinderbox. About half of them addressed him as deputy, the other half as sheriff.

"Howdy Sheriff," Clyde said, greeting Ward as he stepped into the saloon. "Are you here on business or just a friendly visit?"

"Hello, Clyde," Ward replied as he perused the room.

"Looking for someone?"

"I was looking for Coy Prosser."

"He was here, but he and his . . ." here Clyde paused

setting the next word apart, and saying it derisively, "*posse*... left a few minutes ago."

"Do you know where they went?"

"They said they was going after Will Crockett."

"Good Lord, Clyde, didn't you tell them that Will is no longer being hunted?"

"Of course, I told 'em. Half the people in here told 'em, but Prosser wasn't having any of it. He and the others are damn determined to find Will Crockett, if for no other reason than because Will shot Coy with the birdshot."

"Why didn't you stop them?"

"There was five of 'em, all armed, and determined. How was I supposed to stop them, Ward? I could have used my counter rag I guess." Clyde held up the cloth he used in his almost constant wipe down of the bar.

"I'm sorry, Clyde. Of course, there was no way you could, or should, have stopped them. But if, by chance they come back in here, would you get word to me?"

"Sure thing, Sheriff," Clyde replied.

* * *

Worried about the idea of five men going after an unsuspecting Will Crockett, Ward started toward the doctor's office to speak with Anna. She was a good sounding board anytime he was worried about something, and he wanted to talk it out.

"Hello, Ward," Anna greeted with a warm smile. "Have a seat there, I'm helping papa with a patient, but he'll be finished in a minute."

"All right," Ward said, taking the proffered chair.

Ward knew enough about the Crocketts now that, ordinarily he wouldn't be that worried about them, especially when the two of them were together. But this was different. If Prosser and his men came upon Will and Gid, Will would assume they knew he had been cleared of the accusation that he had killed Ty. If they attempted to take him in, or even worse, if they came after him wanting to kill him, Will would have no inkling that that was their intention.

A few moments later, Anna reappeared from the doctor's examining room, a smile on her face. "My, a social visit while you're on duty. To what do I owe the honor?"

"It's not really a social visit," Ward said. "Well, yes, I suppose it is, but I'm worried about something, and I'd like to talk with you about it."

"All right, but how about a piece of pie while we're talking?" Anna offered.

Now it was Ward's time to smile. "You know I can't turn that down."

Ward followed Anna into the kitchen and sat at the table as Anna took a pie out of the pie safe.

"You said you were worried about something." She said as she cut into the peach pie. "What's on your mind?"

"It's that fool Coy Prosser. He's got a posse out looking for Will Crockett."

"I know that. I suppose he doesn't know that Will has been cleared yet. When he finds out, he'll call off the search, and then come back in, don't you think?"

Ward shook his head. "If only that was his thinking."

"Well, does he know what Sheriff Briggs told us or not?" Anna asked.

"Oh, he's been told, but he either doesn't believe it, or he doesn't want to believe it. Clyde says that he's formed his posse again and he's gone back out hunting for Will. Anna, according to Clyde, Prosser says he doesn't intend to bring Will in alive."

"Oh, Ward, you must stop him."

"Believe me I would if I could, but I have no idea where they might be."

"Dunnigan's Grocery Store?" Anna suggested.

"What?"

"If they are going back out, wouldn't they need to get some provisions first?"

A broad smile spread across Ward's face. "Of course, they would. Anna, you are a genius."

Ward left Anna and hurried over to Dunnigan's Grocery Store. He saw five horses tethered out in front, and when he went inside, he saw Coy Prosser standing by the counter as Ernest Dunnigan was gathering his order.

"Prosser," Ward challenged. "What are you doing?"

"I'm buyin' groceries. What does it look like I'm doin'?"

"Are you taking your posse out to look for the Crocketts?"

"We'll only be looking for Will Crockett. We ain't got nothin' agin' Gid Crockett 'less he gets hisself involved."

"Why are you looking for Will?"

"Well, hell, Deputy, I'm just doin' your job for you, seein' as how it don't look like you're a' plannin' on goin' out after 'im."

"Will Crockett has been cleared, Prosser. Sheriff Briggs had clear evidence that exonerated him of any wrong doing. You've got no business going after him."

"He ain't been cleared in no court trial, has he?"

"There's no need for a trial. All charges against him have been dropped."

"Who dropped the charges agin' 'im?"

"I did."

Prosser's smile was without mirth. "Well, now, you ain't no court, are you?"

"I'm warning you, Prosser. Don't you go after Will Crockett."

"All right, I won't go after 'im."

"Now you're making sense."

Again a smile without mirth. "Me 'n the boys is just goin' out deer huntin' is all. 'N you got no right to stop us from deer huntin' now do ya?"

Prosser and his posse stopped just outside of Tilden.

"That feller that was s'posed to have cleared Will Crockett was killt in a bank robbery that took place over in Beeville. I'm figurin' that's where Crockett prob'ly went."

"Crocketts," Purcell said.

"What?"

"It warn't just Will Crocket, it was both of 'em. 'N you damn well know Gid Crockett ain't a' goin' to let us just come in 'n kill his brother."

"That's all right we'll kill both of 'em. We prob'ly should do that anyway, 'cause we wouldn't want that big son of a bitch comin' after us."

"I ain't a'goin'," Purcell said. "The sheriff says Crockett's innocent and that's good enough for me. I wanna sleep in my own bed for awhile."

"I ain't goin' either," Higgins said.

"Why not? I thought we was all in this together," Prosser said.

"It was one thing goin' after 'im iffen he was the one that had killt our sheriff, but now we know he didn't do it."

"We don't know nothin' of the sort," Prosser said. "I don't care what folks is sayin', Crockett killt McMurtry as sure as a gun is iron."

"I won't be goin' either," Jaco said and the three men turned and rode back to Tilden.

"Let the sons of bitches go," Prosser said to Amon Parker and Harry Walls, the only ones who had stayed with him. "They won't be a' gettin' their share of the reward money."

"What reward money?" Parker asked.

"Why, the thousand dollars the state has done put up for Will Crockett, dead or alive." A malevolent smile spread across Prosser's face. "'N I aim to bring the son of a bitch back dead."

Chapter Twenty-nine

Will and Gid had left Beeville right after lunch and reached Oakville by four o'clock that afternoon. During the ride up they had discussed whether they should go directly to Sheriff Algood's office or try and find out a few things before they visited with the sheriff.

"You know the best place to pick up some information, don't you? Everything you might need to know about a town, you can find out in a saloon."

"Plus, get a beer," Will added with a smile.

"Oh, yeah, come to think of it, I'm sure you could get a beer in a saloon as well. I don't know why I didn't think of that," Gid said as he spurred his horse in front of Will.

When the two brothers reached Oakville, they stopped in front of the Hard Knocks Saloon, looped their reins around the railing, then stepped inside.

The saloon was not unlike any of the scores of other

saloons Will and Gid had visited since they had started their drift from town to town after the war.

The serious drinkers were standing, alone at the bar, drinking to push away any of the demons that might be chasing them. There were convivial groups at the tables, visiting with each other, and at a few of the tables, social-izing with one of the young women who were invariably working the saloon.

A poker game was in progress at one of the tables.

"There's a poker game," Will said. "I need to get into that game if I can. There's no better place to find out anything, than in a poker game."

The bartender took their orders, then a moment later handed them two mugs of the golden brew, topped by an inch-high head.

"Bartender, the poker game over there—can anyone get in?"

"That depends," the bartender replied.

"Depends on what?"

"On whether or not you can afford to play. It's a pretty high-stakes game, and you'll have to buy fifty dollars' worth of chips if you want in."

"That's all right, if it's an honest game."

"Oh, it's honest, all right." The bartender looked at the pistol Will was wearing. "But you'll have to check your gun before you sit down."

"That's the rule of the table?"

"My rule," the bartender answered. "I don't want some-body getting' hisself killed in my saloon over a card game. Even if it is a high-stakes game like that one."

"All right," Will said, "if everyone else has checked his gun, I guess I can check mine too. But, if it's all the same to you, I'll just leave my gun with my brother."

"All the same to me, just as long as it ain't you wearin' it, while you're playin' cards."

Will took off his gun belt and handed it to Gid, then started toward the table. There were four men playing, and he was about to ask if they would take a fifth, when one of players decided to leave the game.

"You wantin' to join us, mister?" one of the remaining players asked as he saw Will approach.

"I would, that is if it's all right with all of you," Will answered.

"You have the cost of admission?"

Will put five double-eagles on the table.

"I think that answers my question, mister."

This table was slightly larger than any of the other tables. There were three men at the table and there was one empty chair, vacated by the man who had just left.

"Wait a minute," one of the other players said, quickly. "Before we let you join up with us, how much can you lose?" This was a rather dignified-looking man wearing a tan jacket and a dark brown silk vest. A gold chain stretched across his vest.

"That's a strange comment. Why do you ask?" Will replied.

"You just walked in and none of us know anything about you," the man said. "This isn't a penny-ante game. You might find something more to your liking at one of the other tables."

"I don't see any other games going on," Will said as he looked around.

"Too bad."

"Hold on there, Carl, you got no call to be rude," a gray-haired man said. "He's put down more than enough to play with us. Mister, you're more than welcome at our table. Pete, you're the banker tonight, so take care of our new player."

The man called Pete was about thirty, slim and clean-shaven, with a hawk-like nose. Like Will, Pete wasn't wearing a suit. He reached into the chip box and took out a handful of painted chips. "Red is one, white is five and blue is ten," he explained, sliding the appropriate amount over to Will.

"I'm Ben Urban," the gray-haired man said. "I'm also the dentist here 'bouts, so most folks call me Doc. The banker is Pete Mallory, and the other gentleman is Carl Mitchell."

"What's your name?" Urban asked.

"Crockett. Will Crockett."

"New player, new deck," Doc said. He picked up a box, broke the seal, then dumped the cards onto the table. They were clean, stiff, and shining. He pulled out the joker then began shuffling the deck. The stiff, new pasteboards clicked sharply as he folded the cards in and out. He shoved the deck across the table.

"Cut?" he invited Will.

Will cut the deck, then pushed them back.

Will lost the first hand, but won the second and third, then lost again. After half a dozen hands, he was only slightly ahead of what he had started with.

During the game conversation flowed freely, often interspersed with laughter brought about by one player teasing another. Even Carl Mitchell, who had at first exhibited some suspicion of Will, was now participating freely in the conversation.

Realizing that he was now being accepted by the other players, Will decided that the question he really wanted to ask would not be such an intrusion into the conversation.

"I'm told you had a bank robbery here, yesterday," Will said.

"Bank Robbery?" Doc said. "Yes, you could say that, I suppose. But it's the damndest bank robbery I've ever heard of."

Doc and the others told the story of how the robbers had broken into the Coleman house in the dead of night and forced Edward to go to the bank and empty the safe.

"Then they killed him," Mitchell said, "though thankfully Coleman's wife and child were spared."

"You think it was Jess Felton?"

"Martha said she heard one of them say Felton," Doc said.

"That's Coleman's wife, or actually his widow now," Mallory replied.

The card game continued for about another half hour when Will, who was slightly behind, threw in his cards.

"You men are just too good for me," Will said.

"What are you talking about, you did better than I did," Mitchell said.

"I tell you what, Carl, why don't you join my brother and me for supper? Our treat."

Carl smiled. "I'd be glad to. Where?"

"This is a new town for us, so I don't have any idea where to go. You pick it out."

"Garneau's," Carl said.

"Damn, Carl, you just chose the most expensive restaurant in this part of Texas," Doc Mallory said.

Carl smiled. "I've already seen that I can't beat this man in cards, so I've got to get my money back some way. Wait just a minute, I'll get my hat."

"All right."

After Carl left, Will spoke, privately to Doc Urban.

"I feel a little bad that I won so much money from Carl. Will that put him in any financial difficulty?"

Doc Urban laughed. "Are you kidding? Carl owns the Rocking M Ranch. He's rich as Croesus."

"That's good to hear," Will said.

Garneau's was a surprisingly fancy restaurant, to be in such a small town like Oakville. Two chandeliers provided light, and every table was covered with a white table cloth. They were met at the door by a clean-cut young man.

"Good evening, Mr. Mitchell, will you be wanting your regular table, sir?"

"Yes, Mr. Lewis, thank you."

When they were seated, Will saw that there was already silverware and glassware on the table.

"Good evening, Mr. Mitchell," the waiter said respectfully.

"Good evening, Mr. Gillespie."

"And welcome to your guests."

"My guests?" Carl chuckled. "Well, I suppose you could say that, but that gentleman is to be given the check." He pointed toward Will.

"Very good sir."

Carl looked at Will and Gid. "Gentlemen, shall I order for us?"

"Sure, go ahead," Will replied. "You know the restaurant, we don't."

"Mr. Gillespie, what is the *Plats de jour* this evening?"

"Petit Steak with *pommes frites, tomato provençal, and bordelaise,* sir."

"Then that is what we shall have."

The three men enjoyed a leisurely meal speaking of many interesting things, with no topic being discussed that would be off putting.

When the bill came, Will whistled. "Mr. Mitchell you certainly came a long way toward getting most of your money back."

"I appreciate your generosity, young man," Carl replied.

Will chuckled. "Actually, when you think about, we just enjoyed a fine meal on *your* generosity."

Carl laughed. "I suppose that's right, but I find it hard to believe that you walked into the saloon, sat down with three strangers and played a congenial game of poker for no reason. Would you care to tell me why you are in Oakville?"

Will took a deep breath. "There is a reason why we are here. My brother and I are special deputies," Will replied, "deputized to put an end to Jess Felton and his gang."

"Would it help if you spoke with Martha?"

"Martha?"

"Coleman's widow?"

"Yes, but we would not like to intrude upon her privacy—especially this close to the death of her husband."

"Ed Coleman was not only my banker, but he was a very good friend of mine. I think I can arrange for her to speak to you."

"Thank you, Mr. Mitchell. We would very much appreciate that."

Carl smiled. "We've broken bread together. It's Carl."

Chapter Thirty

"Martha, this is Will and Gid Crockett. They are special deputies, in search of the Felton gang. They would like to talk to you, if you are up to it," Carl said, after taking Will and Gid to the Coleman house, and gaining entry.

"I've told everything I know to the sheriff," Martha replied as she wiped her nose with her handkerchief.

"Yes, ma'am," Will said. "But we'd like to ask you some questions if you don't mind. The first question is, how are you doing?"

"My husband was killed in front of me, and now I am left with a one-year-old child. How do you expect me to feel?"

"I'm sorry, that was an insensitive question," Will said.

Martha shook her head. "No, I was the insensitive one. Please forgive me. I know you meant well when you asked the question. At the moment, I can only say that I'm overwhelmed with what has happened to me."

"I'm truly sorry," Will repeated.

Martha looked directly at Will. "What can I do to help you find these monsters?"

"Tell me as much as you can remember of their conversation, and no matter how insignificant you think the detail, tell me anyway."

She retold how they had come into her bedroom and asked where they could find her husband and then what had happened when they stepped across the hall.

"Felton told Edward that he wanted him to go down to the bank and take out every dollar. Then, when Edward asked why he should do something like that, Felton said that if he didn't do it, he would kill me and our baby."

"You're sure it was Felton?"

"That's what the one called Baker called him," Mrs. Coleman said. "I only heard them say three names: Felton, Baker, and Paxton."

Will nodded. "That's them, all right. Can you think of anything else that might be helpful?"

"Yes, and I didn't even tell the sheriff this, because I was too upset and it just slipped my mind. One of them, I don't remember which one, said that they should stop in Los Lomas and spend some of their money there, but the other said that their cabin was too close to Los Lomas. I don't know if that will be helpful to you."

Will smiled. "Yes, ma'am, you have been a big help. I know it was difficult making you relive all of these details, but you have our deepest thanks."

"Mr. Crockett, find those . . . those . . . sons of bitches and make them pay." She put her hand to her mouth. "I shouldn't have said that. I'm so sorry."

"In this case, Mrs. Coleman, there is no need to be sorry. Your language is perfectly justified. And thank you again for all your help."

"I just hope what I have said will be useful."

"I'm sure it has been, Martha," Mitchell said. "We'll find our way out."

When the three men were standing by their horses, Mitchell asked where they would go next. "There's no question," Will said, "if the cabin they are headed for is too close to Los Lomas, I would say our next stop should be Los Lomas."

"Then Los Lomas it is," Gid replied.

* * *

"Damn, this is the most money I've ever had in my life," Scarborough said after the money from the Oakville bank robbery was counted and divided.

"It ain't quite enough to buy a ranch yet, though," Paxton said.

"'N I couldn't get me no first class saloon with this, neither," Baker said.

"What we need is a bigger bank," Paxton said. "One that has a lot more money."

"You're right, all the banks around here are pretty small," Felton said. "We need to do something bigger. Something much bigger."

"Like what?" Paxton asked.

"Like rob a bigger bank, with more money."

"Bigger banks would be harder to rob, wouldn't they?"

"We've had enough practice, I think we can handle a bigger bank all right," Felton said.

"What bank are you thinkin' about?"

"Cotulla," Felton said.

"Cotulla? Hell, Cotulla ain't that much bigger 'n any of the towns we done hit, is it?" Martin Baker asked.

"Yeah, but the difference is, Cotulla is on the railroad," Felton said. "Look at this."

Felton handed Baker a copy of a newspaper.

Transfer of Funds

Robert Lithgow, president of the Bank of Cotulla announced that on the 15th instant, the International-Great Northern Railroad will be making a temporary deposit of the accumulated funds of three banks before further distribution.

*Lithgow says that the railroad has cho-
sen the Bank of Cotulla as the repository
because of its excellent record of trust and
dependability.*

"That's ten days from now," Felton said. "I doubt that anyone there will be able to recognize us by sight, so I think we should go a couple of days early wait it out in a town that's close by, and maybe have a few drinks and enjoy the women," he added with a smile.

"Wait a minute," Paxton said. "Do you think this here article is true, or is some sheriff setting a trap for us again?"

"Could be," Felton said, "but this time we'll go in knowin' what to expect. We'll be waitin' for 'em. And don't forget, Scarborough and Baker are a hell of a lot better men than O'Neal and Kildeer ever were."

Scarborough smiled. "You got that right. Nobody's gonna take me down in some Podunk town."

* * *

Will and Gid returned to Tilden, planning on going to Los Lomas the next day. They stopped at The Tinderbox for a beer to "wash away the trail dust," and there, they were met by Millie Jean and Sara Sue.

"We'll get a table, if you young ladies will get us a beer and a drink for yourself, and come join us," Gid said.

"Oh, Gid, why you can't even tell you were ever shot. You look like you're getting along just fine," Millie Jean said.

"I am, darlin'," Gid replied. "It just goes to show a bullet can't keep a good man down."

"We've missed you both while you were gone," Sara Sue said. "We didn't know if you'd be coming back to town or if you'd moved on."

"I'd say we'll be around someplace until Jess Felton and his gang are taken care of," Gid said.

"Don't you ever get scared? I mean just the two of you against that whole gang?" Millie Jean asked.

"I don't know, I suppose we would if we really stopped to think about it," Gid replied with a little laugh. "And if we had enough sense to even get scared."

"Finish your beer, Little Brother. We need to go see the deputy," Will said.

"Oh, Ward's the sheriff now," Sara Sue said. "The town council made it official until we can have an election."

"And you won't have to leave," Millie Jean said. "He just came in."

Catching the new sheriff's eye, Will waved him over.

"When did you boys get back?" Ward asked, as he

came to the table.

"About fifteen minutes ago," Will said. "We were about to come down to your office as soon as we finished our trail beer." Will lifted the beer mug for emphasis.

"No need to come to the office. Let me get a beer and I'll join you," Ward said.

"Here, take my seat, Sheriff," Millie Jean said. "I'll get your beer."

"Why, thank you, Fancy. That's very nice of you," Ward said.

For just a second, the name 'Fancy' jumped out at Will, then he realized that to all the customers, Millie Jean and Sara Sue were known as Fancy and Rebel.

After Millie Jean returned with his beer, Ward sat down. "Did you have any luck in Beeville?"

"I'm afraid not, but Sheriff Briggs told us about a horrible killing in Oakville, and of course, the bank was robbed."

"As I heard it, Felton invaded a man's home and then killed him in front of his wife," Ward said. "Now to my way of thinking, that's as low as you can get."

"I agree, but because of that tragedy, we may have gotten our first really good lead," Will said.

"You don't say. What was it?"

"Sheriff Algood arranged for us to meet with the widow of the banker," Will said.

"That had to be difficult," Ward said.

"It was. But she's the one who gave us the lead. She said that they'd mentioned their cabin being near Los Lomas."

"That's entirely possible," Ward said. "I don't know why I didn't think of that before, but that could explain why Los Lomas is the one town in the area that hasn't been touched yet. Are you going over there?"

"We thought we might leave right after breakfast tomorrow. That could put us in Los Lomas by mid-afternoon," Gid said.

"We'll have breakfast together," Ward said.

Harry Walls was sitting at a table that was near enough for him to be able to hear the conversation between the sheriff and the Crocketts. *So, you'll be leaving for Los Lomas tomorrow, will you?* he thought. This was news Coy Prosser would like to hear.

Walls finished his beer, then went to the boarding house where Prosser lived.

"Who is it, and what do you want?" Prosser called in an irritated response to the loud knocking on the door.

"Prosser, it's me, Harry, 'n I got some news you might want to hear."

The door was jerked open. "All right, come on in. There ain't no sense in standin' out there in the hall, yellin' your fool head off."

This was the first time Walls had ever been in Prosser's room, and he was surprised at how unkempt it was. The bed was unmade, there were the stains of expectorated tobacco on the floor, there were dirty clothes strewn about, and there was an unpleasant odor.

"Now, just what is this news that you think I'd want to hear?"

"Will Crockett's in town. Him 'n his brother is down to The Tinderbox now, drinkin' 'n talking to the sheriff."

"What good does that do me? Hell, Haller thinks the son of a bitch is innocent. I couldn't get to him now, without goin' through the sheriff, 'n I'd just as soon not do that."

Walls smiled. "What iffen I was to tell you how we could get to him without Haller bein' around?"

"All right, if you're so smart, keep talkin'."

Walls shared with Prosser, the conversation he had overheard in the saloon, between the Crocketts and the sheriff.

"Yeah," Prosser said with an evil grin. "Yeah, this is good to know."

"The onliest thing there is," Walls concluded, "it'll be both of 'em this time. That big son of a bitch ain't hurtin' no more from the bullet that got 'im."

"That's all right, if we don't take care of both of 'em at the same time, we'd just have him comin' after us later."

"Yeah, I guess that's right," Walls said.

Will and Gid were having their supper in The Iron Skillet when the editor of *The Tilden Free Press* came in. Seeing them, he came to their table.

"Do you gentlemen mind if I join you?" he asked.

"No we don't mind. Pull up a chair, Mr. Jensen," Will said.

"It's Mike," Jensen said. "I was just speaking with Sheriff Haller; he told me that the two of you were in Oakville, and that you met with the widow of Edward Coleman."

"Yes, we did."

"Of everything Felton has done, that seems to me like a new low. Did he actually break into the house in the middle of the night and hold Coleman's wife and child prisoner, while he forced Mr. Coleman to go to the bank?"

"That's what she told us," Gid said.

"God in Heaven, that's the most despicable thing I can imagine. And then, after he complied with their demand, they killed Coleman anyway."

"Yes."

"I know you two are after Felton. I think I speak for every decent citizen, when I say that I hope and pray that you find that piece of filth of humanity and bring him to justice."

"We will," Will said.

ROBERT VAUGHAN

"I like your confidence."

"It's more than confidence, Mike. It's absolute certainty. We will bring Felton and his henchmen to justice."

"Let me see if I fully understand this," Jensen said. "You are saying with absolute certainty, that you will bring Jess Felton and the members of his gang in to face trial and justice."

Will smiled. "Not exactly. I'm saying Felton and his men will get justice."

Jensen looked confused for a moment. "Isn't that what I just . . .," he paused in mid-question as he fully understood what Will had just told him. Then he smiled. "Justice is justice," he said.

"Do you actually want a nightcap?" Will asked as they were walking from The Iron Skillet to The Tinderbox. "Or do you just want to see Millie Jean?"

"I don't care what her circumstances are, Millie Jean is a sweet girl," Gid insisted.

"Gid, you aren't thinking about, that is . . ."

"No," Gid said quickly. "You can put your mind at ease about that." He held up his finger to make a point. "But it isn't because of what she is. It's because . . . well, let's face it, Will. The way we are, the way we live, I doubt if either one of us will ever get married."

"I think you may be right," Will said.

When the brothers entered the saloon, they were met by one of the other percentage girls. They knew this one as Pearl.

"Oh, you'll be wanting Fancy, won't you?" Pearl said to Gid. "Go take a table, honey, and I'll send her over to you."

"Send Sar . . . uh, Rebel as well," Will said.

"Oh, trust me, honey, as soon as she sees you're here, she'll be coming to see you," Pearl said.

Will and Gid were barely seated when Millie Jean and Sara Sue, with broad smiles, came to join them.

"How much does it cost for all night?" Gid asked.

Millie Jean looked surprised. "You want to go up-stairs?"

"No," Gid said. "But I don't want anyone else to go with you tonight either. So, I'll pay you for overnight just to keep you with us for as long as we're here."

"And that goes for you as well," Will said to Sara Sue.

"Oh, well, how long do you plan on being here, if you're paying for all night?" Sara Sue asked.

"It's not actually going to be that long, I'm afraid," Will said. "We're going to have to get up early tomorrow morning."

Neither Millie Jean nor Sara Sue asked why the early rise, nor were they told.

They exchanged stories, many of which brought laughter over the next hour then, shortly before Will and Gid were to leave, Gid put his hand on Millie Jean's.

"If you weren't doing this . . . if you could do anything you wanted to do, what would you do?"

"Oh, Gid, what do you mean?"

Gid realized then that she was reading more into his question than he intended, and he felt bad about that.

"Don't get me wrong, darlin'. The life I lead means I'll never be able to settle down anywhere, and while I don't want to change the way things are, I realize that there are some things that I regret. What I mean is, if you could find any other means of employment, what would it be?"

"Oh, that's easy. Pies."

"Pies?"

"I learned to bake when I was a young girl, and I make very good pies."

"She's telling the honest truth," Sara Sue said. "Lots of times she'll bake a pie for Clyde, me, and the rest of the girls."

"So, if I could do anything I wanted, I would open a pie shop."

"Why don't you?"

"Oh, I'm going to someday, and I'm saving money so I can do it. But I'll need enough to go somewhere else to open it. Because of what I do here," she took in the saloon with a wave of her hand, "so many people know, I don't think I would have many customers."

Gid nodded his head. "I can see that."

"Well, Little Brother," Gid said as he looked up at the clock behind the bar, "it's time we called it a night."

With goodbyes that could best be described as poignant, Will and Gid left Millie Jean and Sara Sue alone at the table.

Chapter Thirty-one

When Will and Gid reached Los Lomas the next afternoon they tied off in front of The Cattle Call saloon, then went inside.

"Yes, sir, gentlemen, what can I get for you?" the bartender asked.

"We'll each have a beer," Will said.

When the beers were delivered, Will put down a ten dollar coin.

"I'll be right back with the change," the bartender said.

"I'd rather have some information."

"What kind of information?"

"What do you know about Jess Felton?"

"I doubt that I know anything that's worth ten dollars."

"Tell me what you do know."

"Only that he's an outlaw, and he's robbed a lot of banks."

"But he's never held up a bank in Los Lomas," Will said. "Is that right?"

"No, sir he hasn't. We've been real lucky on that."

"Are you sure it's just luck?"

"What do you mean, Mister?"

"Could it be that he's keeping Los Lomas as a safe place, somewhere he can come without fear of getting arrested?"

The bartender looked pensive for a moment. "I don't know. I've never thought about it that way. I'll tell you this, if he's ever been here, I don't know nothin' about it. But he could 'a been here without me knowin', on account of I don't have no idea what he looks like."

"He has a pock-marked face and a drooping eyelid," Will said.

The bartender shook his head. "No, I don't reckon I've ever seen anyone that looks like that."

"Sure you have, Tony," one of the saloon kibitzers said. "Clay Evans comes in here from time to time, 'n he looks like that."

"Yes, but these fellers are lookin' for Jess Felton, not Clay Evans."

"Evans?" Gid said. He looked at Will. "Are you thinkin' the same thing I'm thinkin'?"

"Dan Evans," Will said.

"No, Clay Evans," the bartender said.

"Do you have any idea where Clay Evans lives?"

"No, I don't. Someone said he has a cabin near here, but I don't have no idea where," the bartender said.

"Thank you," Will said. "That's worth the ten dollars."

"We need to go talk to Dan Evans again," Gid said as they were leaving the saloon.

"We should have gone back to talk to him long ago," Will agreed.

Just as the two men started to untie their horses, a bullet struck the hitching rail as the sound of a gunshot reverberated through the street. There was a watering trough to either side of the hitching rail and Will dived behind one, while Gid took the other. Their movement was followed by three more gunshots.

"There's more than one of 'em, Little Brother," Will called across the space between them.

"It looks like we've found Felton," Gid called back.

"No, it looks like he's found us."

There were three more shots and because they were separated, Will and Gid were able to locate them.

"There's one up behind the false front of the tobacco store," Gid said.

"And I'd say one in the loft above the livery and one behind the corner of the leather shop," Will added.

There were several more shots exchanged but because all the shooters were well protected, no one was hit.

"Gid," Will called. "Do you remember Abilene?"

"Damn, Will, are you sure you want to do that?"

"I think it's the only way we're goin' to get them out of there. Can you think of a better idea?" Will asked.

"Damn, it's a hell of a note when that's the best idea we can come up with. All right, who do you want to go first?"

"We'll go together. They won't know which shot to take first and that'll give us a little advantage."

"All right."

"On three," Will replied. "I'll count."

Will and Gid cocked their pistols and got ready.

"One, two, *three!*" Will counted.

At the count of three they stood up, then ran out into the street.

"You sons of bitches, I'm going to . . ."

As expected, the three men they were in a gunfight with, opened fire.

"Arrgh! Gid, they got me!" Will shouted as with a grimace of pain he went down.

Gid went down in the same fusillade. The two men lay belly-down in the middle of the street.

"Coy! We got 'em! We got 'em!"

Coy? Coy Prosser? What was he doing here? Will wondered as he and Gid lay motionless in the middle of the street.

"Let's get down there and finish them off."

That was Coy Prosser as Will recognized his voice.

"You two take care of the big son of a bitch—Will Crockett is mine," Prosser said.

"Are you ready, Gid?" Will asked quietly.

"I'm ready."

"I'll give the word. Take the one on your side."

When Will fell, he had made certain that his face was turned in the direction of the shooters. He watched as one man came out from the corner of the leather shop and the two others climbed down from the top of the tobacco store and from the loft of the livery. Coy Prosser was the one who came down from the livery loft. Will had no idea who the other two men were.

He waited until the three men were in the street, and close enough together to make an easy target.

"Now!" Will shouted and he and Gid jumped up.

"What the hell?" Prosser shouted, startled by the sudden activity of the two men he thought were lying dead in the street.

"Drop your guns!" Will ordered."

"Shoot 'em, shoot 'em!" Prosser called and he and the two men with him raised their guns to shoot.

Will fired twice, Gid fired once, and the three men went down.

When Will and Gid went over to check on them, they saw that all three were dead.

"Did you see that?" someone shouted.

"Damndest thing I ever seen."

"Why you reckon them three opened up on those two men like they done?"

"We'd better go see the sheriff and let him know what happened," Gid said.

"No need for that," Will said. "Unless I miss my guess, here he comes now."

A tall man with a black handle-bar moustache came walking quickly down the road. There were at least a dozen men coming with him, and another half-dozen or so who had come out into the road from near-by buildings.

"What happened here?" the sheriff asked.

"You should 'a seen it, Sheriff Woodson!" someone said. "These two men here come out of the saloon, 'n these three that's lyin' in the road commenced a' shootin' at 'em."

"Why were these men shooting at you?" the sheriff asked.

"I'm not sure, but they may have been a posse out to get me."

"A posse? Who are you?"

"I'm Will Crockett. This is my brother, Gid."

"Will Crockett? Mister, I've got paper on you. You're the one that killt Sheriff Ty McMurty!"

Will shook his head. "I didn't do it, and I've been cleared."

"I ain't heard nothin' 'bout you bein' cleared."

"Send a telegram to Sheriff Haller in Tilden. He'll tell you I've been cleared."

"What's to keep you from running off while I'm waitin' on the telegram?"

"You got any coffee in your office?"

"What kind of sheriff's office would I be runnin' if I didn't have 'ny coffee."

"All right, my brother and I will wait with you in the sheriff's office until you get a reply," Will said.

Sheriff Woodson stroked his moustache with his finger as if contemplating Will's suggestion, then he nodded. "I'll just take you up on that offer."

Half an hour later Sheriff Woodson returned to his office, carrying a telegram. Gid was playing checkers with the deputy, and Will was reading a copy of *Harpers Weekly Magazine*.

"Sheriff Haller says you're tellin' the truth," Woodson said. "He also says that you're lookin' for Jess Felton."

"We are," Will said. "Do you have any information we can use?"

Sheriff Woodson shook his head. "I wish I did."

"I was hoping we might get a lead by coming here, but I guess not," Will said. He kept to himself that the man calling himself Clay Evans might be Jess Felton, because he wanted to talk to Dan Evans before he went any further with that information.

"You'll be goin' on then?" Sheriff Woodson asked. "The reason is, there might be some others a' huntin' you that don't know you been cleared. 'N I'd just as not have no more shootouts in the street here."

Will chucked. "I'd as soon not had this one."

"I don't blame you. From what the others have been tellin' me, you two was shot at first, 'n was damn lucky you didn't get yourselves killt."

"That could very well be," Will said. "Thanks for the coffee."

"Any time. I wish you fellers good luck, 'cause I've got me a feelin' you're gonna need it."

Chapter Thirty-two

"I got a telegram from Sheriff Woodson telling me about Prosser and his posse," Ward said when Will and Gid walked into the sheriff's office.

"See Little Brother, I told you a telegram would get here before we did."

"Maybe if we had ridden a bit faster," Gid suggested.

"What?" Ward said, then when he realized the brothers were teasing, he laughed.

"I hated the way it turned out. Apparently, Prosser was after the bounty that was put out on me, and he must not have known I'd been cleared," Will said. "If he would have approached us, rather than ambushed us, it might have turned out differently."

Ward shook his head. "No, the son of a bitch knew you'd been cleared, that's why half his posse left him. But it didn't make any difference to him."

"I'm sorry it turned out the way it did," Will said.

"It seems like Prosser held a grudge because you loaded him up with birdshot," Ward said. "But what about your trip to Los Lomas? Did you find out anything about Felton?"

"I'm not sure, but we may have something. I need to talk to Dan Evans again."

"All right, I'll go with you," Ward said.

When the three men rode down to Clark and Hopkins freight line, Dan Evans was supervising the loading of one of the wagons.

"Mr. Evans," Ward said. "I wonder if we could talk to you."

Evans looked at them for a moment as if contemplating whether or not he wanted to talk, then he called out to one of the men.

"Jim, would you handle this loading manifest? I need to talk to these gentlemen."

"Sure thing, Mr. Evans," a short, muscular-looking man replied.

"Come on, we can use Mr. Clark's office," Evans invited.

Fred Clark was sitting behind his desk and he looked up when Dan and the others came in.

"Mr. Clark, would you mind if we used your office for a few minutes?" Sheriff Haller asked.

"Sure, go ahead," Clark replied. "Take all the time you need. I'll just get out of your way."

"Thanks," Will said.

When Clark was gone, Dan turned to Will.

"It's about Jess, isn't it?" Evans said. "Is he dead?"

"It is about Felton, but he isn't dead. At least, as far as we know, he's not."

"All right then, what do you need?"

"Are you aware that Los Lomas has had no problems with Jess Felton?" Will asked.

"Yes, I know that," Evans said.

"From time to time one of the saloons in Los Lomas has been visited by someone who matches Felton's description," Will said. "He identifies himself as Clay Evans."

Evans was quiet for a moment so long that Will wasn't sure he was going to reply. Finally, taking a deep breath, then exhaling audibly, Evans responded.

"Jesse Clay Evans. For awhile, after he come to live with me, he took up his mama's maiden name which, as she was my sister, was the same as mine. He was Clay Evans 'till he went off on his own, then he took his daddy's name 'n started callin' hisself Jess Felton."

"Mr. Evans, we have a suggestion that he may be using a cabin that's near Los Lomas," Gid said.

Again, Evans was silent for a moment, then he sighed. "That would be my sister's house on the Nueces River."

"Where on the river?"

"There aren't any roads or towns, or even no other houses nearby." Evans walked over to the wall where there was a map of McMullen and LaSalle Counties, then he put his finger on the spot. "It's right here, where the river makes it deepest curve."

"You've known where he is for some time, haven't you, Mr. Evans?" Will asked.

"I. . ." Evans started, then after a long pause, he completed his sentence. "I've suspected that might have been where he was hidin' out, but I've kept quiet about it because he is my blood kin. But, God forgive me for doing that because my keeping quiet about it has caused some good people to be killed. But blood or no, he has to be stopped."

"Mr. Evans, I don't hold your reticence against you," Ward said. "You've redeemed yourself."

* * *

When they reached the cabin, they stayed out of sight as they examined it. There was a little lean-to building behind the cabin, that they assumed was a stable, but there were no horses in or around the building.

"Maybe they're keeping them somewhere else," Gid suggested.

Will shook his head. "Huh uh, I don't think so. Look around, there's no other place close enough to keep horses. That's where they would keep them."

"There aren't any there," Gid said.

"I think the cabin's empty," Will said.

"What? You mean this has all been a wild goose chase? That this isn't where Felton's been staying?"

"That might be the case. Let's go down and see what we can find."

Moving cautiously, Will and Gid approached the cabin. Will looked in through the window.

"It's empty," he said.

"Damn! Then it has been a wild goose chase."

"No, wait, I can see some bedrolls on the floor. Let's go in and have a look around."

It took less than a minute to ascertain that though the cabin was empty at the moment, it was definitely being occupied. In addition to the bedrolls, they found a smoked ham, canned food, and a tin of coffee on a shelf near the stove.

"I wonder where they are," Gid said.

After looking around, Will saw a newspaper lying on the table. He perused the front page for a moment.

"Ha! I know where they are," he said. "Or at least, where they're going to be four days from now."

Sheriff Seth Talbot was as big as Gid, and the two men eyed each other as if they were mutual members of some secret society.

"And you're saying that Jess Felton is going to be here," Talbot said.

"That's what we think."

"Today?"

"Today's the day the money's supposed to get here, isn't it?"

"It is," Talbot replied. "The schedule is that the train will arrive at ten o'clock, and the money will be in the bank by ten fifteen."

"I expect Felton will hit the bank before ten thirty."

"How many are in his gang, do you know? The railroad's supposed to have some sort of guard, but you can't count on them, and my deputy's out of town right now."

"We think there are four of them, but if you'll deputize my brother and me, we'll handle it for you," Will said.

"Two of you? Against four of them?"

"We can do it," Will said.

"Very well, hold up your hands," Talbot said.

Will and Gid did so.

"You're deputized. What next?"

"Where's the best place to keep an eye on the approach to the bank?"

"Well, the best place," Sheriff Talbot started, then he chuckled, "the best place would be the Calico House. That's a dress shop right across the street from the bank, and Marie has a big front window so you can see everything. I don't know how you fellas would feel about waitin' in a dress shop though."

"I think it's perfect," Gid said. "Felton's not likely to take a look through the window of dress shop."

Talbot nodded. "You've got a point. But promise one thing. When you confront Felton and the others, don't make the dress shop a target."

"We won't," Will said.

"Come with me, I'll let Marie know what's going on."

On the morning of the fifteenth, Jess Felton woke up in the bed of a whore. Felton and the other three had been in the town of Dull, Texas, for four days, spending two nights at the Two-Bit Saloon, and two nights in the Water Hole. They availed themselves of the soiled doves in both saloons.

Felton dressed quickly without disturbing the woman who had told him her name was Delilah, then stepped out into the hallway and knocked on the other three doors.

"All right," Felton told the others over breakfast. "It'll take us about three hours to get to Cotulla. That means we'll get there around ten-thirty. By then, the money will be there and safe in the bank, or that's what they'll think. We'll take the money, go back to the cabin, divide it up, 'n go our separate ways. It'll be better if we don't none of us never see each other again."

Marie had put chairs out for Will and Gid, and brought them coffee, but otherwise left them alone. They had watched as the railroad guards escorted the money to the bank, and once it was deposited, they had walked back to the waiting train and pulled out.

Will checked his watch. "If we're right we won't have long to wait." He took a drink of his coffee.

"You're right about that, Big Brother, here they come," Gid said.

"Marie, if you have a cellar or a store room, I think you and your customer should think about going there, now."

"What? Why should we do that? Seth didn't say anything about your being here that would be dangerous."

"I think it's just best that you take shelter. And don't come to the front of the store until all the shooting has stopped."

"Shooting?" Marie gasped.

"Please," Will said. "Go back there now."

"Come on, Alma, let's do what the man says," Marie said anxiously, herding her customer to the storeroom at the back of the store.

Felton and three more men came riding into town. Will and Gid knew Martin Baker, and they recognized Ben Scarborough from the description of his nose. The other one had to be the one known as Paxton.

"Wait until they dismount," Will said. "They'll be less likely to ride away when we challenge them."

The four men stopped in front of the bank. Felton, Baker, and one other man dismounted, then handed their reins to the fourth rider.

"Now!" Will said, and he and Gid ran out through the front door.

"Felton, you and your men drop your guns!" Will shouted. "You're under arrest!".

"What the hell?" Felton yelled. "Kill 'em, kill 'em!"

The man who was still mounted, put his hands up.

"Baker, you cowardly son of bitch!" Felton shouted, shooting his own man.

That was the first shot fired, then as the four horses, all of them now riderless, galloped away, Will and Gid exchanged gunfire with Felton, Paxton, and the man with the deformed nose.

Will felt a burning sensation in his shoulder as he saw Felton go down under his gun. The other two men went down immediately after, and the volley of gun shots that had filled the street with thunder, came to a halt.

Now, hesitantly, many of the town's citizens, caught

by surprise by the gunfight, began to come out of the building in curiosity. Some were hesitant, not knowing Will and Gid, but seeing two men still armed.

Sheriff Talbot came running up the street then, and seeing that he didn't appear worried, their own fears were alleviated.

"I would never have thought that two men could take out the Felton gang," the sheriff said, "but I saw it with my own eyes."

"Well, you've never seen the Crocketts, Will and Gid, in action, and now you have," Gid said as he helped Will to his feet. "Are you all right, Big Brother?"

"It takes more than a bullet to take a Crockett out," Will said. "I think it's time for us to get out of here."

Epilogue

"I appreciate you men coming to the wedding," Ward said to Will and Gid during the reception celebrating his marriage to Anna.

"The only reason we came is so your new father-in-law could patch up my arm," Will said.

"Ha, some wound," Gid said. "It's not much more than a scratch. Now I had a real wound," he added.

"The only difference between us Little Brother is I was fast enough to get out of the way, while you were so slow that you got hit hard in the leg."

"Who's not fast enough? You may have noticed that you were the one that got shot last week. I didn't."

"Will you two ever quit arguing with each other like that?" Anna asked with a little laugh.

"If we didn't argue with each other, we wouldn't have anything to talk about," Will said with a broad smile.

From the wedding reception, Will and Gid went to The Tinderbox Saloon.

"Oh, my, don't you two look elegant though," Millie Jean said when she came to greet the two.

"Millie, get your sister and join us at the table," Gid said. "We want to talk to you before we leave."

"You're leaving?" Millie asked with a pained expression on her face.

"You've known all along that we wouldn't be staying," Gid said.

"I . . . I know, it's just that, I'm going to hate to see you two leave."

"Get your sister and join us," Gid said.

"Shall we bring you a couple of beers?"

"That would be nice."

Will and Gid took an empty table and were alone for a moment as they waited for Millie Jean and Sara Sue to join them.

"Will, are you sure you don't mind doing this?" Gid asked.

"Little Brother I'm glad to do it," Will said. "And proud that we can."

A moment later the two sisters joined to the two brothers, Millie Jean carrying a beer in each hand and Sara Sue carrying the tea that they would be drinking.

They were both smiling, though there was a sense of melancholy to their smiles.

They exchanged a few greetings, then Gid addressed Millie Jean.

"Are you serious about wanting to open a pie shop?"

"Yes, very serious."

"What would Sara Sue do?"

"She would be with me. When we get money saved, we'll buy it together and be partners."

"How much longer before you'll have the money you'll need?"

"I don't know how much longer. Maybe a year. Maybe more than that."

"Would a thousand dollars speed up the process?"

"Are you kidding if we had a thousand dollars, we could leave today," Millie Jean said.

Gid smiled, reached into his pocket, and pulled out a banded stack of money.

"You've got another thousand dollars," he said. "This is from Will and me."

"What?" Millie Jean shouted so loud that everyone in the saloon looked over toward them. "Are you serious?"

"You see the money lying there, don't you?"

"Oh, oh, oh!" Millie Jean shouted, and she ran around the table to hug Gid, as Sara Sue hugged Will.

"That was for Katie," Gid said as the two rode away.

"I know it was. You may be big and ugly, Little Brother, but you are a good man. Where to next?"

"I don't know," Gid said. "I've been thinkin'. We both got shot this time. Maybe our luck is running out. What would you say about getting out of Texas for awhile?"

"Sounds good to me. Where will we go? East or West?"

"Let's flip a coin and see." Gid took a gold piece out of his pocket and flipped it in the air. It came up heads. "All right, heads it is. We're heading West."

"West? I didn't hear us say heads meant West?"

"Well, I did the flippin' and I did the callin'. So West it is."

If You Liked This, You Might Like: Lou Prophet: The Complete Series, Volume 1

THIS PROPHET IS RIDING TO HELL AND BACK.

Lou Prophet's life as a bounty hunter has taught him one rule: You don't stop riding till the job is finished. Prophet is repeatedly caught in bloody crossfires and he is determined to show the outlaws that justice doesn't always wear a badge.

Join the bounty hunter as he searches for a gorgeous showgirl, chases down a brutal gang, protects his partner at all costs, escorts a Russian noblewoman on an Arizona trail and captures stage-robbers!

"A storyteller who knows the West."—Bill Brooks

Lou Prophet: The Complete Series, Volume 1 includes – The Devil and Lou Prophet, Riding With the Devil's Mistress, The Devil Gets His Due, Staring Down the Devil, and The Devil's Lair.

AVAILABLE NOW ON AMAZON

About the Author

Robert Vaughan sold his first book when he was 19. That was 57 years and nearly 500 books ago. He wrote the novelization for the mini-series Andersonville. Vaughan wrote, produced, and appeared in the History Channel documentary Vietnam Homecoming.

His books have hit the NYT bestseller list seven times. He has won the Spur Award, the PORGIE Award (Best Paperback Original), the Western Fictioneers Lifetime Achievement Award, received the Readwest President's Award for Excellence in Western Fiction, is a member of the American Writers Hall of Fame and is a Pulitzer Prize nominee.

Vaughan is also a retired army officer, helicopter pilot with three tours in Vietnam. And received the Distinguished Flying Cross, the Purple Heart, The Bronze Star with three oak leaf clusters, the Air Medal for valor with 35 oak leaf clusters, the Army Commendation Medal, the Meritorious Service Medal, and the Vietnamese Cross of Gallantry.